JT Wilson grew up imagining
be as debonair and dashing a
talented and acclaimed as David Bowie. Somewhere
along the line and probably due to his own clumsiness
and indiscipline, the ambition stalled, buried beneath a
mass of hair-dye, glitter, cheap drum machines and a
conversational style combining his posh education, the
guttural vowels of his coastal Northern hometown and
his fondness for Bill And Ted and Teenage Mutant Ninja
Turtles. Since then he has variously found work as a
church caretaker, a debt collector, a rock singer and a
professional wrestling manager. He lives in Coventry.
'Cemetery Drive' is his first novel.

Cemetery Drive

J.T. Wilson

Cemetery Drive
By J.T. Wilson

First Published in the UK in August 2010 by Hirst Publishing

Hirst Publishing, Suite 285 Andover House, George Yard, Andover, Hants, SP10 1PB

ISBN 978-0-9566417-2-4

Cover Illustration by Die Booth
Cover Design by Robert Hammond
Edited by Jack Dexter

Printed and bound by Good News Digital Books

Paper stock used is natural, recyclable and made from wood grown in sustainable forests. The manufacturing processes conform to environmental regulations.

www.hirstbooks.com

"I take it that no man is educated who has never dallied with the thought of suicide."

William James

Chapter One

(I)

It was 11.13 when the doorbell rang at Conzeula Martinez's house, but she knew when she answered that the time had somehow become irrelevant, because while the man at her door had caught her ill-prepared and his arrival was unexpected, she had been awaiting him for much of the last twenty years.

'What's up? You were expecting someone else?' Zan asked, giving off the cheery glow of an icicle.

'You can't come in now,' managed Conzeula, by way of response, 'I've got guests.'

'Groovy. You know, I love parties. And I'm sure they won't miss you.' Zan stepped past Conzeula and entered the house.

The lounge was accessible through a dimly-lit corridor masquerading as a hallway and was a museum of 1970s fashion, a mausoleum in orange and brown. Zan stood in the middle, sweeping his gaze across tasteful knick-knacks and family photos in black and white crammed on top of broken machines and a low-power gas heater. The room was far from warm, a long way from glowing and barely hospitable. It hung with the odd stench of cabbage and musty decay common to rooms of this nature. Somehow the stale fug overrode the cold, the icy feel being pushed down to an undercurrent by the impenetrable atmosphere. It seemed to Zan that this was how the old stayed warm, at least, those in this social class: by never opening windows and stewing in their own dense mist, the memories of long-forgotten fires and meals delivered by home help. Most of the time, their minds were roughly similar to the decor.

There was no sign of the claimed guests. Not that they would have operated in any realm Zan moved in any more anyway; but it wasn't that easy to fool him.

'Sweet joint you've got here, Mrs M,' said Zan by way of conversation. 'You know, this is the sole physical memorial of your time on Earth, the one thing you'll leave behind. I bet you're stoked. Anyway,' he added, turning to leave, 'we'd best get going, don't you think?'

'I can't leave,' Conzeula insisted. 'I've got a very important visitor coming in a moment and I can't afford to go anywhere in case they come. I don't understand what you're doing, coming here and scaring an old-'

Her flow was crudely interrupted as she followed Zan's pointing finger to the body slumped in the corner. Somehow, anything that she said from there would have been irrelevant. Defeated, she picked up a handbag and joined Zan.

'So where did you say we were going?'

'Hartlepool. I'm late for an appointment.'

(II)

At the same time, alarms howled, sirens screamed and megaphones spouted Hollywood clichés. As the crowds milling around wondered whether to crane their necks for a better view of the events unfolding and of the protagonists becoming visible amongst the mass of uniforms, or whether it might be a wiser idea to flee in terror, the departure of one woman was barely noticed. Not now anyway.

(III)

Oblivious to any developments that might be going on outside, or indeed may have happened at all in the last seventy five years, the magisterial court radiated austerity. Electric lighting struggled to illuminate mahogany walls and polished flooring, affording the court a severity hardly deserved by the minor scrapes and disputes which populated it.

A session was in place today as any other weekday. This particular debate was brought to court by Nicolas Aster, who was sat here slumped in a wheelchair as his lawyer, Paul Kendall, provided the case for the defence. Unusually for a case conducted at this level and in this court, a certain amount of media interest had gathered. The press box was, for once, filled with more than the usual local journalist obliged to diligently write a transcript of the day's events for a quarter-inch of newsprint. This case had a certain novelty to it that had tickled the fancy of even the national media.

'I admit that I myself thought this case extremely unlikely when I first took it on,' the Hon. Kendall was saying. 'However, when I looked into it further, I had to concede that Mr Aster raises a valid point.' He failed to mention at this point that the further research which he had done had been largely research into Aster's bank account. Research into the contrast between the potential fees that he could recover (and had already recovered) from the case and the possible damage to his credibility as a lawyer for taking on such a ludicrous case. Research into yacht prices.

'Under the terms and conditions of the Consumer Credit Act, any credit providers must provide a signed agreement for the services provided,' he continued. 'Such a contract providing goods and services is consistent throughout all legal precedence. Those unable to provide legal documentation which proves that goods, services or credit facilities were provided and that the client was aware of the terms and conditions of such before entering into the agreement have found themselves in a position where the agreement is null and void.'

'My client Mr Aster was not in receipt of any documentation of this nature when he agreed to occupy the physical body within which he currently operates. As you can see from my client's current physical condition, this body, if it were to be sold in a shop, would be considered ineffectual, defective. Yet because the body is provided for my client at the point of birth, it is considered inevitable and irrevocable. One cannot simply transport Mr Aster into a new body, gentlemen; advances in medical science are yet to progress that far. So it goes to follow that any providers of this physical vessel, having metaphysical powers which extend beyond the capacity of human knowledge, would already have been aware of the defects before attachment of the soul to the body. Not only that, it goes to follow that they did so without providing the client with any documentation agreeing to this! Therefore it is a reasonable argument that the agreement is null and void and that any steps taken by God or his authorised representative, Death, to recover the soul from the physical body are irrelevant.'

'Objection, your honour,' came a voice from the back of the room. 'This is clearly absurd reasoning by the Honourable Mr Kendall on behalf of his client.'

'Let it be noted for the record that an objection was raised at this point,' the magistrate rasped, disappointed as he had been on many occasions before that his voice lacked the necessary bass to add a Shakespearean gravitas. 'Who is it that has the impertinence to interrupt this session?'

Zan smiled, holding his hands out as he approached the court. 'You'll pardon my lack of grace, Your Honour. It was not my intention to hold this court in contempt. I'm sure, however, that we're obliged to hear a case for the defence in this hearing? Well, it looks like it's my job to offer it. I'm Zan, by the way.'

'You come representing God?' asked the magistrate doubtfully, looking at Zan's leathers and jeans combination and imagining that God would normally have sent a better-dressed representative to a courtroom.

'No, I don't represent God, come on,' scoffed Zan. 'God is totally all over that free will concept, remember? As far as he's concerned, what humans do is their own business and they can argue it among themselves. People have sued God before without an appearance by the Almighty. No, I'm here to represent the metaphysical entity with most to lose in this case– I'm here to represent Death.'

'If I might bring the court's attention firstly to the notion raised that-'

'Objection, Your Honour,' Kendall interrupted. 'We have no way of proving that this man is who he claims to be. Without any obvious legal qualifications this man could easily be a charlatan!'

'It's true that I have no legal qualifications in solicitation – sorry, is that the word?' smiled Zan genially. 'What can I say– my particular department of the afterlife was being legally challenged, so I had a vested interest and I was in the area. Anyway, you're wanting me to prove that I'm from the afterlife and not just some random guy. I guess it's the fact I don't wear a hood and carry a scythe, right? What can I say – they had none in my size. But I suppose a quick parlour trick's probably cool. Hey, court official– what time was it when I came in?'

'11.13, sir,' reported the official, checking his record.

'Okay, and I've been here about, what, five minutes? Are we all in agreement that to be able to collect all of the souls of the dead, given the volume of the population, Death would have to exist outside of time: that is, existing on a different metaphysical plane to collect the dead? Think of it like Santa Claus, except collecting rather than delivering.'

'Santa Claus doesn't exist though, does he sir?' asked the official.

'Can it be noted for the record that in a court hearing I was asked whether Santa Claus exists or not?' asked Zan, rolling his eyes. 'Anyway, the idea of time stopping but our conversation continuing would indicate the appearance of a metaphysical being, right? So what time is it now?'

'Still 11.13 sir- but that's impossible!'

'There we go. Check your watches if you like, your digital phones, whatever timekeeping you've got on you, they'll all say the same thing. Now can we please get on with it? I know that time's frozen, but I don't have all day, you know.'

Zan addressed the magistrate. 'Now if I can begin with the argument raised by the honourable gentleman that there's no legal documentation evidencing the attachment of the soul to the body. Well, if you look in the Registry of Births, Marriages and Deaths there's a birth certificate for Mr Aster. I dunno, maybe I don't get your quaint English customs but that seems like a pretty conclusive legal document, right? I guess it's more like a receipt than a pre-contractual notice, though. Perhaps you could consider it a warranty. Then there's the claim that those who attached the soul to the body were aware of the defectiveness of the body and that they should have notified the client. Well, sorry Nick, and it sucks. But they can't all be winners, and there's a certain amount of personal responsibility here.'

'I mean, I'm no medic, but the big C is a hereditary condition, you know? The validity of contracts has been called into question many times, I'm sure, by lawyers arguing that their client was a minor at the time of signing. Until legal documentation can be signed by one in sound mind to do so, the parent or legal guardian must sign in their place. I mean, how old would this guy be when this contract would have had to be signed? Less than zero, right? So if a contract signed by someone under 18 won't hold up in court, how would you expect a contract signed by a pre-birth to stand up? It wouldn't– so it's parental responsibility again and hey, it was them who brought you into the world Nicky boy, take it up with them.'

'Then I could get into the whole issue of this court being viewed in the eyes of God and acting as God's representatives on Earth so querying the nature of the infinite one would have to question the concept of law itself, and the issue of having to swear on the Bible and how that features plenty of detail about souls being attached to physical bodies and separated from them but you know, it's irrelevant.'

'Why is that?' asked Kendall.

Zan scrunched his face up. 'Mainly because Nicholas Aster died at 11.12.' He pointed to the chair, where Aster was slumped lifeless.

'I'm sure you guys over there from the media will point out how ironic this death is, but I'll let you guys worry about that and I'll worry about what I need to do.'

The court returned from its time vortex and people rushed around the body of the deceased. On another plane, Nicholas Aster and Zan looked on.

'It was a rough deal I had, you know.'

'I know it was,' said Zan, 'and I'm sorry. But it's over now. Come on, it's time to go.'

(IV)

It all seemed so worthless, so insignificant. Here was Robbie Adams, who had, at one time, the potential to change the universe, reduce the very fabric of existence to its bare essentials and rebuild it in a new, glorious

14

fashion. Robbie Adams, whose name would be whispered in hushed tones of awe, whose name would appear on streets, whose likeness would be etched in stone and marble across the planet. Robbie Adams, the myth, the legend, the conquering hero. What news could equal him in significance, in stature, in importance? What groundbreaking, Earth-shattering news could even reach him and be dismissed with more than an insouciant shrug or contemptuous yawn? Yet here it was, all around him. Hundreds of articles about tea parties and family fun days and industrial tribunals. Bland advertisements for discounted chicken fillets, cheap cruise liner holidays and relaunched hair salons. And he– yes he, Robbie Adams, the indestructible, the peerless, the unfathomable!–was actually being expected to not only acknowledge its existence but to actually deliver this news. He was expected to cram it through the doors of the ignorant and unnecessary, where it would await its deserved fate, lining cat litter boxes and repainted bedrooms.

Not that it was important to Robbie what was happening in the world or how his genius was going to waste, of course. For Robbie had decided, after a period of reflection and research, to kill himself. It was patently obvious even at seventeen years of age that this world would never come to accept him, never welcome his genius or even understand it. His grades and social standing were irrelevant here. Mozart was performing allegros and andantes at five years old. Michael Jackson had had, what, five Number Ones? at this age. And what had Robbie Adams done at this point? Nothing, nothing.

He wondered whether it was just that he wasn't meant for these times. In a world of social networking, downloaded blockbusters and viewer voting, acting, which was the only thing he could ever do, could ever wish to do, was becoming an increasingly lost art. The theatre had spent most of the century becoming an increasingly fringe pursuit regarded as stuffy, regarded as equivalent to opera and art galleries. There had been serious arguments in his peer group about which action hero was the better actor. Given their complete inability to do anything other than look moody and fight, this was the sort of thing that made Robbie think that his talent was anachronistic and would never be used productively. Even at the pinnacle of his powers he would have to hope for a leading role as a moody comic book superhero for anyone to regard him with the respect he clearly deserved.

It seemed like such a waste. Anything had to be better than this: the days spent muddling through whatever shit gets thrown, hoping to recede into the background to avoid attention, to avoid being singled out. The evenings spent wondering how to kill time before bedtime and invariably squandered in ways that never made sense. The nights plagued with insomnia hoping that the next day doesn't throw up anything quite as horrible as the last. Oblivion, when you're in that position, seems increasingly like such a noble ambition: so exquisitely simple and yet so conclusive. Nothing would matter any more, nothing would hurt, there would be no time to waste, or to dwell on a lack of achievement, or to wonder whether anything of consequence would ever happen, ever, or whether there was merely a directionless and hopeless future. Oblivion, finally. Thank God. Thank God.

With the decision made to commit suicide, the only question was how to die in a distinctive and memorable manner which, crucially, didn't hurt too much. Stuff like overdoses and hanging seemed so mundanely familiar, so obvious and overdone. Not that Robbie had known anyone who'd ever committed suicide, of course, but he had read books, watched films, hell, watched *CSI* and he knew which ways were boring and cliché and those, my friend, were them.

He'd considered slitting his wrists– fairly simple and quick– then walking into the sea, but would that be how he'd want to be found? Facedown with a mouth full of sand? Besides, the sea was full of salt, you idiot, how would that feel in your last moments pouring through your open wounds? Sure, it would be over pretty rapidly, but you'd still look like a chump and the pain would be horrible.

He'd simply have to find another plan, something that drew attention to his artistic, sensitive side but was also something he'd wanted to achieve, a middle finger to thwarted ambition and a heartless world. Then, all of a sudden, in a flash of inspiration while listening to late night radio and trying to ignore the fact that he had to be awake at 7am for college, he had it. By 2am, he had a complete list of ten potential locations and methods. Ten places to die. He would visit each one in order and the first one which came across as ideal, he would do. Sure, it would cost, but since he didn't have anything else lined up for his future, what difference would that make?

The only thing that stood in his way was that, at this point, he didn't have any money to spend. The best things in life may very well be free, but it seemed that the best modes of death were not. He had needed work, which is why at whatever Godforsaken time of the morning this was, he was not enjoying some well-earned sleep but dragging two bags of papers around the suburban cul-de-sacs. Two different local papers had recruited his services and sometimes he thought that they would cruelly deny him of his fate by causing him to drop dead of exhaustion or overloaded weight. Still, at the end of the day a job was a job however badly paid or socially insignificant and, compared to flipping burgers or cleaning toilets, this was a walk in the park.

Past the old cynics watching warily out of their windows, nothing better to do but stare at their world all day, Neighbourhood Watch stickers in the window apparently a disclaimer for spying. Down the driveways of the 'NO FREE PAPERS' brigade, half of whom he delivered to anyway; I mean, fuck it, these bags were heavy and if the old bastards cared that much, they could write a five-page complaint letter to the paper and bring some sunshine into their dreary lives.

Through the letterboxes populated on the other side by furious dogs. Ignoring the furious dogs treating the intrusive paper as if the criminals and murderers it depicted were not merely newsprint but real living entities, ready to thieve flatscreens and DVD players and murder their beloved master while they were at it. Down the same old route and still hundreds of these bloody things to go.

Down Mangle Street with its long-abandoned industrial warehouses, now used as offices for some feeble trade journals, trying desperately in their writings to disguise the fact that Britain was no longer the industrial empire it once was, to disguise the irony of their writing from a disused factory about how productive Britain's industry remains— and aha, suddenly there was a turning he'd never seen before. A turning

18

seemingly long forgotten and now overgrown with the brambles and nettles who'd clearly seized the opportunity of space greedily, but there it was, a whole load of previously unexplored houses. Many were the sort of shambling, rundown houses which were no doubt populated by similarly shambling, rundown people, living on the precipice of total collapse. Cemetery Drive. They would never read these papers, of course, probably barely acknowledged that we were now living in the future, their houses doubtless a museum of porcelain dolls and old smoke. But hell, did Robbie want to carry these papers all day long, or did he want to finish dumping them and get on with his day?

He continued down Cemetery Drive, pushing through rustic, rusty gates and crazy paving which had now become crazy enough to be sectionable, and then, then a door opened in Cemetery Drive and Robbie Adams was changed forever.

(V)

Zan drove the bus at unfathomable speed, with extravagant nonchalance, and tried desperately to ignore the woman in his ear, who, as is the wont of old women, had insisted on chatting to the driver throughout the journey.

'So, like I say, can you tell them when you get back that there's been a mix-up? I mean, I don't know whether

19

you've got the authority to make the changes or not, but surely it can be checked,' the old bat was saying.

Zan sighed. 'Look, lady, this isn't some sort of administrative error, y'know? This is the incorruptible, omniscient depiction of your entire life that we're monitoring here. It's not a typo, or a blunder. It's not some sort of computer crash where we've gone to the wrong house and we'll rectify it immediately. Everything we're going from here – everything – is based on your actions, your decisions, your memories. Things you remember, things you've forgotten– or tried to, at least. It's not like, 'oh whoops, looks like we've got CONCHITA Martinez's records here, damn, sent Zan out by mistake there, my bad,' we're running a completely different system here, do you understand, a *completely different*– aw crap, missed the turning-' and the bus wrenched round at impossible angles and careened to a stop outside a bank.

There was chaos there: broken glass and what appeared to be smoke, but was more likely condensation and steam from sprinkler systems, filled Zan's view. The passengers on the bus– for there was more than Conzeula Martinez and Nicholas Aster, this had been a full day's work and an extremely productive one– remained impassive, nervously contemplating their own fates or else staring doe-eyed, cattle-like. In all cases, they were displaying the interest in the outside world that one might expect from a lampshade. It didn't matter. This sort of thing no longer affected them and never would again. Zan, meanwhile, remained equally unaffected. He had done jobs like this before, hell, jobs far worse than this if we're being honest. He was desensitized now. No doubt he was in for a complete horrorshow when he got there, but it's difficult to feel horrified at humanity in this job.

Keep your eyes on the prize, demonstrate 100% focus, all that jazz. That's how he'd got where he was today, for better or for worse. *Let's get this show on the road.*

He stepped out of the bus, the mess around him– barricades, tape, debris –having no effect on his passage. Police and bank staff repelled the curious and the media but ignoring him, letting him enter. The crowds saw the scene of devastation but did not see Zan as he stepped neatly past traumatised survivors and the wreckage of what, up until an hour ago, had been just another branch of a high street bank. Zan barely saw them, either. He knew exactly what he was looking for here, knew the exact co-ordinates to the square inch, had never seen his bounty but knew exactly what it was and where to look, and ah, a step to the left at this ATM and   . . . There was nothing there.

There was nothing *fucking* there.

Maybe that missed turning had delayed him, caused him to miss it, it was already being moved– but that was impossible. He didn't run late; not because of outstanding time management, but because it simply was not possible. Nor did the information he'd been given ever make mistakes. This just did not happen. Had not happened, could not happen. How could it not be there? He was collecting souls from dead bodies! So where the hell was the dead body and, more importantly, where was the soul? And if there was meant to be a soul to collect and all of a sudden they were nowhere to be seen.

This was bad. This was so, so bad.

Chapter Two

(I)

The woman at the door in Cemetery Drive clung to the doorframe as if a tornado was blowing through the streets. Her hair was black by nature and flame-red by design, a blonde streak running aimlessly through it, and heaped around her head with no thought to sculpting or even taming. Below, mascara and lipstick attempted desperately to escape their original placement, while a shapeless dress in a vile shade of purple made it impossible to gauge the figure underneath. The image was topped off by a long cigarette holder, adopted presumably in a tribute to Audrey Hepburn but lacking the essential ingredients such as class and poise.

Robbie thought it was the most beautiful thing he'd ever seen. It was at a point like this that a certain dignity, elegance and poise was needed. A suave opening line, and this girl– this *lady* would be putty in his hands. Of course, it's hard to do that when your jeans are still coated in yesterday's mud, your shirt was bought from, and should have stayed in, the charity shop and you're carrying three hundred local rags, but–

'What do you want?' the woman whispered urgently, interrupting Robbie's mental browse through the library of James Bond lines.

'Express delivery?' offered Robbie, weakly.

'They're after me. They're everywhere. We don't have much time.'

'What? Who's after you? What do you mean, we?'

'You'd best come in. Quickly!' hissed the woman, as Robbie dithered.

He obeyed. His parents, of course, would warn him about the dangers of stepping into a stranger's house, but his parents were not here. Besides, the worst that could happen is death, and that's small threat to someone who's fundraising for a once-in-a-lifetime trip around the world to commit suicide.

He'd naturally expected the surroundings to match perfectly with the image of fallen grace that had answered the door. A natural decadence, drapes and beanbags making up the décor, overflowing ashtrays, empty bottles of absinthe, everything broken or dissolute. Possibly a scrawny cat or two acting as company. Perhaps a smashed photo of the woman and a long-lost love, thrown to the ground at 4am during a bender of whisky and pills, shortly before the police were called by the neighbours.

Instead, everything was neat. A light, airy, pleasantly furnished lounge opened up to an immaculate kitchen. There was tasteful art in equally tasteful frames adorning the tasteful walls. There were no photos, smashed or otherwise.

'Probably not what you expected from a home furnished by the woman you're looking at, huh,' remarked the woman, flicking ash into a mug. 'I dunno, I think it's that whole 'an Englishman's home is a castle' thing, y'know. Plus, however messed up the world is– huh, however messed up *I* get– I know that I can come home and everything's fine. I can control *that* much.'

Robbie thought of the undisciplined state of his room at home, about how the chaos in his room reflected the

23

chaos of his life, and nodded. He didn't know what to say; he barely knew how to talk to girls, and this lady was impossibly old to him; like 45. It was like talking to one of your Mum's work colleagues or something.

The woman moved to a leather sofa and sat down. 'Come on, join me, why don't you. It's OK, I don't bite. Haven't bitten for the last ten years at least. I'm Alexa Ribiera,' she added, by way of introduction, as Robbie sat warily down next to her.

'Robbie Adams. It's a pleasure to meet you, Mrs Ribiera.'

'Firstly, it's *Miss* Ribiera, thanks, and call me Alexa. None of this parent-teacher meeting stuff here. Alright, I'll make this blunt, Robbie. Today, I was at a bank and missed being shot and killed by inches. I literally dodged death today.'

Alexa paused for reaction. Robbie knew he should say something, but had no more idea of what to say than if he'd have been invited to speak at a quantum physics conference. It was later in the day than he'd thought, nearly midday; even so, for Robbie, this was still a horribly early time to have to be awake on a day when he didn't have to go and pretend to be interested in education.

'Wow. Well, it's a close shave alright, but it mustn't have been your time,' Robbie managed. He accepted a cigarette from Alexa as she relit.

'Not my time, huh. What do you know about death, kid?'

'I know death some,' mused Robbie. He was thinking of his grandfather's death, how 75% of the knowledge he had of his granddad came from that day, that funeral and that wake. A wake where people struggled to remember the names and pertinent information of distant family members who'd probably seen the deceased once in the last year, if that. He thought of how his grandmother's awful singing, when she concluded her eulogy with a version of 'Ave Maria' which brought tears to the eyes for all the wrong reasons, had made the funeral even more of an ordeal than it should have been. *That's something for the suicide note,* he thought, *specifications about who does and does not sing at the funeral.*

'You don't know death any, babe and quite frankly, I'm in the position of not having experienced it myself– not my own, anyway,' said Alexa, looking at him. 'But I know, for fact, that it was my time to die. I should have been shot right there and I wasn't. The way that I avoided it, though: I know that I've done it, that I've dodged the bullet, but I'm not convinced that's going to be forever. I know that now Death will be coming for me, hunting me down, and I don't have time for that sort of thing. If I can dodge it I'll be free. I've avoided my death and, providing I play my cards right, I should be able to live forever.'

Robbie frowned. 'How do you know any of this is going to happen? I mean, are you sure?'

'Do you have a camera?'

Robbie was completely confused now. 'Well, I've got one on my phone, I think.'

'Take a photo of me.'

'What?'

Alexa rolled her eyes. 'Look, if it matters that much to you, you can delete it straight away, alright, just do it.'

Robbie took a photo.

'Woah, that is weird.'

The photo was of the sofa and the walls behind it. Alexa was nowhere to be found.

'Spooky, huh? I've been erased from the Earth already.'

'Are you a ghost?'

Alexa took his hand. 'Do I feel like a ghost? Now. How you feature into this is as follows, because God knows I didn't invite you in to discuss the doings of the local mayor or whatever other crap is in that paper. Right now, I'm running low on allies I can trust, particularly ones who ain't Goddamn cowards. You're young, look healthy enough, and at your age, probably have a clear enough conscience. But when it comes down to it, are you able to look Death in the face and say, there's no way you're going to take Alexa Ribiera?'

Robbie was thinking that when he saw Death, he was more likely to offer himself up with relief than defy the Reaper. But either way, that counts as not fearing Death, right? Plus, while this whole situation was completely weirding him out, what was weirdest about it was how there was something . . . I dunno . . . hypnotic about Alexa, the way she crossed her legs, hell, her legs full stop, the way that she'd decided to put her faith entirely in someone who only crossed her path by delivering papers. What was the worst that could happen?

'When Death comes, I'll make sure the right decision is made,' said Robbie, carefully.

'Good boy,' said Alexa, extinguishing her cigarette. 'I knew I opened the door to you for a reason. Now, to test whether you've got the fight in you that I need.'

And she kissed him.

(II)

Zan careened the bus into Limbo, an impossibly empty space which was neither good nor bad. He could afford to be a careless driver in this environment: space and time were difficult to imagine, or even describe, in this place to a first-time visitor: luckily, however, one time would be all you'd ever need in Limbo. For Zan, however, trapped eternally between Heaven and Hell, he was a full-time resident, he knew full damn well where everything was, and his place was just over there on the left, or was it the right?

He was pissed off. He'd gone to collect a soul, which should have been floating around detached from its body, but neither the body nor the soul were there. Somewhere, there was still an unclaimed soul floating around. Was it alive, or was it lost for good? Should he report it to the big man, or try and sort it out himself? If he reported it to the big man, how would that affect his job?

He didn't know what to do. He'd just have to get on with the task at hand first, get rid of this collection of cadavers, then worry about whether or not a soul had escaped. He made a perilous three-point turn which sent passers-by scrambling as if their eternal souls were somehow at risk.

Ambling up to the coach as it made its erratic parking manoeuvres in Limbo were Beelzebub and Astaroth, part of the Seven Satans, the chain of command in Hell one step below Lucifer. Beelzebub looked like a conventional portrayal of a demon, shaven head, goatee bead and Anton LaVey dress sense. Astaroth was younger, more vibrant and full of nervous energy, dressed in a Byronic combination of frilly shirt and even frillier hair. Zan and his peers, whatever their official description, were generally referred to as banshees, and through regular business dealings Beelzebub and Astaroth had come to know Zan well, and Zan happened to get on well with them. As a teenage rocker, Zan had always dreamt of partying with the Devil, but his mother would have been proud to know that he recognised, and was on friendly terms with, various saints and angels. Such apparent dichotomy was inevitable when positioned dead-centre between good and evil. Death was neither good nor bad, it was just an eternal constant. In Zan's experience, sometimes it had been good and sometimes it had been bad; but here on the other side, it was just a job.

'I was just thinking I hadn't had enough diabolical dealings recently, guys. Thankfully you turned up, eh? Anyway, what brings you up here?'

'It's these Adherence To Policy meetings,' sighed Beelzebub. 'Ever since *someone-*' he cast a glance at Astaroth -'told Lucifer that God doesn't attend these meetings because he considers himself ineffable, enigmatic, dedicated to pure enlightenment and holiness and that Heaven was left to the domain of the angels, Lucifer decided he was evil, full stop, and therefore no longer required representation. It's that whole yin/yang stuff, y'know, the infinity of good versus the infinity of evil. If there's good, it logically follows that there's evil. If there's an extremity of pure holiness and light then there must be an extremity of pure evil and darkness. That's his logic anyway.

'Anyway, the point of this is that someone's gotta do it if Lucifer can't be arsed to attend, with the result that Ash and I have ended up doing all these meetings.'

The Adherence To Policy meetings were semi-regular, though interminable, meetings amongst Heaven and Hell's primary movers and shakers. They were meant to ensure that Hell was playing by the rules and, perhaps less pressingly, that Heaven wasn't being too lenient. There also needed to be regular updates on 'good' and 'bad', since, say, stoning people to death for mocking the bald didn't necessarily fast-track the bald-mocker to Hell any more. Among recent thrilling topics of discussion had been: should unbaptised children all go through Purgatory? And should all witches go to Hell, if they use their powers for good? Beelzebub hated them. Zan held the suspicion that the ATP meetings were heaven for those on the side of good who enjoyed administration and meetings and were enforced primarily to create Beelzebub's own personal Hell. The people he knew in Heaven were forever coming out with nonsense about how 'productive' and 'constructive' these meetings were. Beelzebub and Astaroth, on the other hand, tended to use much shorter adjectives – four letter adjectives to be exact. It didn't surprise Zan at all that both God and the Devil had managed to weasel out of them.

'It's insane, y'know,' whined Beelzebub. 'I was worshipped as a God in ancient times. Lord of the Flies and all that! And now where am I? Forced to do His Royal Highness's dirty work, wasting time – well, I say time, you get my drift – time I could be spending creating evil instead.'

'Hey, at least you did better than some ancient gods,' interjected Astaroth, 'I mean, look at cats. Strutting round like they're the cock of the walk in Egyptian times. Feared for having the key to the underworld. Fast forward 2,000 years, there they are wearing collars, shitting in trays,

29

eating biscuits with a high ash content. You know this shit? I mean, how do you reach the decision that what cats need in their diet is a nice, healthy dose of ash?'

There was a pause.

'Well, maybe you can ask the inventor of cat biscuits when he gets down here,' remarked Beelzebub, dryly. 'Anyway,' he added, turning to Zan and hoping to quench Ash's factoids, 'I don't suppose there's any chance that we might get to see you at work today? Ash has been harassing me forever to see your work again. Besides, he's never been onboard a plague wagon.'

'Look, the correct term is soul train. But yeah, sure. Come on board.'

'I think people are always kinda disappointed that the Grim Reaper couldn't be with them personally,' mused Zan, as they boarded the coach. 'Some of them are so set in their ways, I just tell them I'm Death to shut them up. Y'know? I mean, I guess I am, by proxy, right? I'm not sure it helps though, and it really bums them out – I mean, even more than they already are – when they find out they've gotta go by coach.'

'Yes, I noticed that,' Astaroth intercepted. 'I heard you had 200,000 people a day coming in here. Couldn't you use a quicker method of transport?'

Zan thought. 'Well, we've just got the soul train – we've got bigger versions for the genocides and mass death, all that fun stuff. Death himself uses the Astral Plane though!' He laughed, which made Astaroth look over at Beelzebub for clarification. Beelzebub merely shrugged. Not noticing, Zan continued, 'I suppose it's the quickest method of transport we have, large-scale. A bit more classy than just shoving them in, I dunno, a lorry or something, y'know? Long-term, it wouldn't solve the perception that public transport is for losers.'

The carriage gave the impression of being a congested Victorian affair from the outside, but upon entering, the demons were surprised to find that it was a spacious modern looking affair. More legroom than usual, and a selection of fine wines in a cooler by each table – clearly everyone had a smooth final journey. That said, Beelzebub half-wondered whether this was just a trick of the imagination or if everyone's perceptions differed: it wouldn't be the only place in the afterlife based on illusion. Even then, he supposed, time and space were the same thing and if one existed outside time, one existed outside space as well, so why wouldn't the soul train be bigger on the outside?

'Good afternoon, everyone! My name is Zan, and I'm your conductor on this journey. We've now reached your final destination, and you'll be disembarking shortly. We're joined this afternoon by two guests, our current Southern representatives, Beelzebub and Astaroth. Now, if you've led a good life free from sin and full of virtue, yadda yadda, don't sweat it, you'll be getting your wings automatically as soon as you step off the train. But if you don't get your wings, I'm afraid Bub and Ash here will be taking care of your future.'

'Looking forward to getting to know y'all better,' grinned Beelzebub. Zan rolled his eyes – typical Bub, stirring it.

Zan moved down to the end of the train, past the hundreds of souls looking nervously behind him at the tall bearded man and his shorter, prettier colleague who accompanied him. The demons stuck their thumbs up in mock jauntiness. Anything to be a jerk. At the back of the final carriage was a padlocked door. Zan took a bunch of keys from his pocket and leafed through the keys idly.

'I'd hang onto something if I were you, guys,' Zan muttered to Beelzebub and Astaroth. 'That's if you weren't planning to return to Hell right away.'

As Beelzebub and Astaroth hung onto nearby rails, Zan picked out the key and unlocked the padlock.

'I wish you well, and if you haven't been good, be careful!' Zan laughed, then opened the door.

The door backed onto a huge cylindrical tube, which blew a gale into the train, sending souls sprawling. Astaroth and Beelzebub fought their way to the front to watch the spectacle as the souls, having battled against hope to stay on the train were finally blown into the cylinder. Beelzebub was amused to note one old salt grabbing a bottle of wine on the way to almost certain damnation.

To the disappointment of the demons, a surprisingly high number were blown upwards, their wings appearing on their backs as they flew up towards Heaven. Those who didn't were sucked down into Hell, where the demons and their minions waited to receive their guests. There was a third option, which merely blew souls sideways into Limbo but, due to various tightening on regulations and negotiations with the North, very few souls ever went in there. Beelzebub, Zan had heard, hated the idea of Limbo. Spending the rest of eternity experiencing nothing at all was Hell for those who chose to live in Hell.

Zan wandered along the train, ignoring the gale and removing the last few survivors who, somehow, had managed to hold on throughout the hurricane that tore through the train. He noted to his disappointment that some couples were being separated for eternity, and was even more saddened to find a child clinging onto the bottom of a table. Zan figured she couldn't have been any more than eight.

'Hey, little dudette, it's time to go,' Zan said gently, crouching to meet the child.

'But I don't wanna,' sulked the girl. 'Nobody else is here. I want my mummy.'

'I'm sure you'll be reunited real soon, right? But you're not gonna meet her any time soon if you keep hanging round here. C'mon, think of it as, I don't know, a reverse slide. Go on.'

The girl, acquiescing, stood up and was blown into the gale to take her journey. Zan liked children (and in a wholly innocent way), but in this job, he was never glad to meet them.

The transition, though: now that was something to behold. The rapture. The change in these poor saps' faces as they realised their destiny, already you can see it and they're not even there yet, the look of sudden revelation and, depending on their circumstances, shock or awe. Nobody thinks they've done enough to get into Heaven, nobody thinks they've been bad enough to get into Hell. A blinding flash, and they're gone. Limbo is empty.

Zan, dazed by the rapture no matter how many times he'd seen it before, pulled himself together. He took a pack of cigarettes from his pocket, lit one and started smoking anxiously. He held his other hand up as the demons opened their mouths to protest.

'I know this is just a simulation of a cigarette, a remnant of my physical needs for a soul that has no need for them,' he explained to Beelzebub and Astaroth. 'But shit, let me have my deceit, I need it. Yeah, yeah, yeah, it's my oral fixation, blah blah blah. I know, but if you wanna get Freudian on me, I'm not interested, okay?'

'What do you need to smoke for?' asked 'Bub. 'I imagine corpse collecting in the plague wagon isn't exactly a demanding job, or a stressful one. You turn up, pick up the dead, move on. You can freeze time, so that's no boundary. I mean, what's the problem?'

'The problem is when one of the motherfuckers escapes!' squealed Zan. 'I went in to collect one stinking soul in a bank shoot-out in this shithole English town, and the ever-loving thing had fucked off!'

Beelzebub and Astaroth stared at Zan.

'One . . . escaped?!' gasped Astaroth, burying his face in his hands. 'Do you have any idea what the consequences of this kinda thing even are?'

'Are they bad?' said Zan, hazarding a guess.

Astaroth threw his hands up, agitated. 'If a human soul can escape the crushing inevitability of death at the exact point that they're supposed to die . . . I mean, there's only one death per person scheduled, right? So if they miss that meeting . . .'

'. . .then they've discovered the secret of immortality itself,' finished Beelzebub. 'And if one person's discovered immortality then you're sure as hell likely to find that becomes two people pretty quickly. Then four. Then, I don't know, sixteen. You've got to hunt down that escapee, before it's too late and humans have eternal life forever and ever.'

'But how do I even go about finding the one?' asked Zan.

'Well, have you tried looking?' asked Beelzebub sardonically. 'And failing that, work out how it's done,

34

and hunt down the humans who've helped them, because they definitely weren't working alone.'

'You're right, of course,' sighed Zan, heartened by his ancient friend. 'But where do I start looking?'

Chapter Three

(I)

What more can be written about the first time you make love, how many words could possibly romanticise the occasion any more than it needs? What purpose depicting, in any lurid detail, the congress Robbie and Alexa found themselves engaged in? For Robbie, it was a big deal, but he knew when it was over that, lacking comparison, he couldn't tell whether it was good or bad. He couldn't tell whether he had been ready or not and whether Alexa enjoyed herself or merely pretended to: certainly, he didn't dare ask.

Clothes strewn across the bedroom like the wreckage of a hurricane, hair more ruffled and disjointed than before (and it was, in both cases, unkempt enough already), there lay Alexa and Robbie, under crumpled sheets. Robbie had always hoped his first time would be in some opulent, candle-lit bordello, with silk and satin everywhere. Possibly leopard print sheets or white tiger stripes and gold trim on the bedposts. Some romantic piano music perhaps playing in the background in the soft-focus setting of his imagination. He had yet to distinguish between class and crass. Instead, the bedroom was in a light, airy blue with neat skirting boards and pine furniture. A small CD player, a Booker Prize-nominated paperback, a cheap-looking lamp and an alarm clock were all that adorned the small chest of drawers which sat besides the bed. Again, there were no photographs, no hint as to the past or present of Alexa Ribiera.

Robbie supposed that it was better this way, that it wasn't a fumble in some back alley or broken-down club toilet. That at least this way, he wasn't having to look at posters of pop stars or Hollywood starlets or, who cares, Rafael Nadal or something while waiting for the girl to sweep her bed free of pink lipstick, mobile phone bills and images printed from Facebook or MySpace or whatever. He thought of his own bedroom at home. It was still – still! plastered with road signs, pull-out posters from Nuts and Kerrang!, miscellaneous postcards, newspapers clippings and other junk that had amused or meant something to him, and the map of the world he liked studying while plotting his own untimely demise.

He could never show Alexa his room.

Alexa was reaching for an ashtray hidden under her bed, drawing a packet of cigarettes from some hitherto-concealed hideaway. Robbie tried to work out whether the expression on her face indicated that the act they'd recently engaged in was magical and glorious or mundane and trivial. It was impossible to tell. He accepted a cigarette.

'So tell me about yourself,' Robbie said, as Alexa lit his fag with a lighter that had magically appeared from somewhere. 'I want to know, I dunno, *everything*.'

Alexa looked amused. 'You mean my main appeal isn't my exotic mystique?'

Robbie frowned, embarrassed. 'Well, I guess in a way,' he mumbled, 'but if I'm going to protect you and guard you with my life, I'd like to know more about you. Like, what do you do, for example?'

Alexa grinned. 'Guard me with your life? You're so dramatic, Robbie. Not that this isn't fabulous or anything,' she added quickly. 'As for what I do, I worked at a Bureau de Change. I always wanted to see the world, but I never dared. I heard about the wars in Africa, the drugs in the Caribbean, the kidnapping and human trafficking in Europe, the gun crime of South America, the . . . in China . . . the . . . oh, it just seemed so dangerous, so fearsome. What time is it, by the way?'

Robbie told her.

'Guess it's too early to break out the wine, even on a special day like meeting you,' she yawned. 'Anyway, I know this will shock you under the circumstances, it shocks me that I'm confiding this shit to someone I just met, but I'm terrified of death. Always have been. So that was my concession to travel, to exploration: allowing other people to do so by giving them currency. Safe job. No real promotion opportunities, not much prospect, sure, but on the other hand, steady work with no stress. I've played it safe my whole life, everything that I've done, based on fear.'

Robbie thought that all the smoking and drinking she'd been doing was hardly playing it safe – more like playing into Death's hands – but said nothing. Even Robbie, who was hardly Casanova, knew that it was too early in the relationship to risk taking the piss, in case it turned out Alexa offended easily and threw him out.

'I've stayed home a lot. Kept the place immaculate, of course, but it's always been a sanctuary, a refuge. I saved money well, spent according to my means, stayed home a lot. I tried to avoid rough clubs or dodgy guys, most of the time anyway. At one point I even considered setting up a business from home, online trading, that kinda thing, but,' she shrugged, waving her hands vaguely, 'what's the point? What do I know how to do, huh, other than selling foreign currency? I mean, you can't do that from home. Besides, having a job helped with that all-important social interaction, work. Fresh air, time out of the house . . . ah, all that good stuff.'

Robbie tapped his cigarette into the offered ashtray. 'Why are you saying this past-tense? You could always go back to work. We're trying to escape death here, but how many people have ever died at a bureau de change? I mean, that's why you chose that job, right?'

He got out of bed, now fizzing with the effervescence of adolescence. 'I mean, I could stay with you here forever, but it's not going to work. Death is coming for you Alexa and if he is, this is the first place he's gonna look. We have to get out of here. Go somewhere safe. Somewhere where we aren't going to meet him.' He took Alexa's hand. 'We go now.'

'Well can we at least get dressed first?'

'NOW.'

(II)

'The frickin' bitch gave me the slip again!'

Zan had been frustrated. He'd checked out the file of this Alexa Ribiera. Christ – I mean, man (no cuss-words that relate to God or the Devil, it's all good as far as we're concerned, remember), the chick was dull. A real stay-at-home. No husband, no wife, not even a close contender

39

there: it was unlikely that she would have split town with someone and more likely she'd been hanging out at home. So of course, he'd taken the logical route and taken a cruise down Cemetery Drive and the motherfucking broad had blown the joint. No clues, no leads. The trail had gone cold.

So here he was explaining all this to Beelzebub and Astaroth again, to their mild amusement. They needed something to cheer themselves up, after all. They'd just endured an interminable session discussing whether witch doctors should or should not be eligible for Heaven and whether tribesmen in remote outposts who'd never heard of monotheism were deserving of Hell for believing in more, or less, than one God.

'How is it even possible for you to just miss someone, when you can pick any time and place ever and just go straight in there?' asked Ash.

'I picked the wrong time,' muttered Zan, who hadn't thought of that and was embarrassed about it. 'She's off the radar, what can I say? I'm just guessing here, you reckon you can do better, Satan Twins?'

'Hey, hey, stay cool, banshee. Just make sure Gabby and Chris don't find out about it. I mean, our lips are sealed, obviously; we're friends, you know that. We're tight. But-' and here Astaroth looked around confidentially, although probably to ensure he had an audience rather than to ensure nobody was listening – 'they'd be straight up there yapping to Our Father and St Pete because it's the Morally Right Thing To Do.'

Zan frowned. It was impossible to tell with these two. Sure, they were mates and all. On the other hand, they were mendacious, exaggerating demons: at least you could rely on honesty with the other side. Beelzebub particularly was the right-hand man of Lucifer: he'd give you false information just to screw with you and to stick a middle finger up to Heaven. This said, the advice was almost certainly correct: he knew full well that Bub and Ash were complete hypocrites and would be blabbing to Lucifer, but he couldn't imagine Lucifer giving a crap. If God was to find out, on the other hand, you could guarantee he would be putting some Old Testament-style self-righteousness on Death, which would only reflect badly on Zan and ruin his chances of escaping Limbo any time soon. In fact, it could be worse and Zan could be lumbered with Hell for the rest of eternity. The afterlife was a political nightmare. To get advice from Heaven or from Hell he felt like the chick from *Labyrinth:* he had to decide which of the gargoyles was lying.

'Look, man, I don't know what to do here. I mean, it's not like I've got many clues here, y'know? You must have seen stuff like this happening before: give us some ideas.'

'Hey, don't get us into it,' said Astaroth, stepping back in an exaggerated manner. 'We're the forces of evil, and you're the neutral ones, right? You can't take sides – everything's gotta be regulated and agreed, right?'

'Look, don't rag on me, Ash, I don't have time for bullshit. Just tell me what's going on, otherwise we're going to end up with a situation where everyone on Earth can avoid death and nobody in Heaven and nobody in Hell gets any new souls.'

'Well played, Zan,' Beelzebub smiled, while Astaroth glowered, suitably chastised. 'OK, the main things that people have tried to avoid death are magic and technology. Magic's obvious – immortality spells, incantations, bathing in virgins' blood. In terms of technology, you've got to be looking at cryogenics, Botox, anything which reverses or cancels out ageing. Of course, it's never worked, it's tilting at windmills: but imagine if you could combine the two? Cryogenics *combined* with immortality spells, or injecting virgins' blood directly into your face: it sounds ridiculous, but how are any of us supposed to know? None of us have tried it, after all. We're in the metaphysical dimension and you guys have obviously been caught napping rather than keeping your finger on the pulse. Um, metaphorically speaking I mean.But who's to say nobody's decided to combine technology and magic and coffin-dodge that way?'

'He's right,' added Ash. 'Nobody's going to figure this out on their own. But whoever's taken it upon themselves to sidestep death, whoever's decided to achieve immortality by simply missing their death, they're smart. And they're going to be busy thinking of new ways to sidestep you. You're not exactly short of time: I mean, it's a relative concept and you can go wherever you like and whenever you like, but you're best off looking before the Jolly Grim Giant finds out and starts sharpening a scythe with your name on it, y'know?'

Zan ran his hands through his hair. 'So you're saying I need to find someone who knows technology and who knows magic . . . and in the meantime the girl I should be pursuing is getting further and further away? She could be a million miles away now!'

(III)

They were sat in the Salonium, awaiting their turn for the barber on duty. However, they weren't sat aimlessly reading three-month old copies of Hello! or Nuts, nor idly half-listening to news, weather and sports updates on the radio. Instead, they sat in spacious seats eating popcorn and watching an art-house biopic of Millie Kennedy, the singer whose rootsy jazz/folk gained her a large following among suburban housewives after her death, but who had been largely discredited in the last five years. Robbie, who had been a fan of her first two albums for years, could not remember why that was.

The Salonium was a hybrid business venture created by two businessmen who saw their businesses on the downturn. It combined the humble barber's shop – seemingly in terminal decline in favour of the swish hair salons which offered loose mullets and peroxide tints (Alexa's own hair dyeing was done at home in a budget exercise which proved another futile effort to give life to her hair)- and the arthouse cinema, the style itself swallowed up by multiplexes and art centres. While still only doing modest income, the Salonium was still an improvement, financially, on the previous successes of the would-be entrepreneurs, while, importantly, saving money on overheads. The previous barbers shop had, somewhat unhygienically, been sold to a chain of coffee shops. Plus, it stopped customers getting bored during the previously soulless wait for a haircut.

In this instance, the wait for the barber's chair, situated smartly in the middle of the back row to prevent pundits having their view interrupted, didn't bother Robbie at all.

Making out with a chick in the back of a cinema was a rite of passage, more or less, one which he intended to fulfil.

Alexa, however, was restless. 'Robbie, what's all this about?'

Robbie explained the Salonium's history. 'Just be grateful we're not watching *Sweeney Todd*.'

'What, the demon barber of Fleet Street? You reckon they'd be that crass?'

'Oh, not because of the hairdressing link. Just 'cause that movie sucks.' Robbie turned back to the screen, reaching an arm around Alexa.

'Anyway, I mean, why are we in a cinema to start with, if the Grim Reaper is hovering around?' asked Alexa. 'We're sitting ducks, aren't we?'

Robbie turned back to Alexa It didn't matter too much if he missed a few seconds of an interview with Millie Kennedy's parents or whatever else was onscreen. Probably another vacuous kooky-pop airhead banging on about how influential Kennedy was to her work, thus sucking up to the dead and flagrantly shilling her own output in one breath. Time was when Millie Kennedy had meant a lot to Robbie, although, while he still loved the albums, he had lost faith in her story a while back. Why he'd become disillusioned with her, he couldn't remember. Perhaps he'd just grown out of her. Or given up on the idea that anyone had ever felt the way he did.

'Well, it certainly isn't for the movie quality, that's for sure. It's as simple as this: it gives us time to think and to regroup in a place which isn't renowned for its body count. I mean, how many people can you think of who died in a cinema?'

'129. Moscow, 2002.'

44

'What? Do you just collect weird death statistics or something? I thought cinemas were like Disneyland, where nobody ever dies onsite.'

'Actually, that's a myth too. Eight people have died at Disneyland.' When Robbie stared, Alexa added, 'Girl's gotta have a hobby. Can't be too careful out there. Is there an ashtray in this place?'

A tap on the shoulder indicated Robbie and Alexa were next in the barber's chair. Alexa took the first step up, for another fruitless effort at trying to discipline her hair. To the barber, it was akin to asking a landscape gardener to cultivate a jungle.

'Anyway,' Robbie said, taking an adjacent seat, 'aren't most deaths caused in the house? And you haven't had too much of a problem with staying at home, Little Miss Agoraphobe.'

Alexa kept her head straight, staring at the screen as the barber valiantly battled against a much stronger foe. 'It's all about safety in the home. My electrical appliances are all in warranty and my roof checked for leaks. My bedroom, as you'll remember from earlier, is on the ground floor, to prevent any late-night falls. You can't guarantee that sort of safety anywhere else outside the home, so I choose to leave it rarely. Happy?'

'OK, whatever,' growled Robbie. 'Either way, we can't keep ducking and weaving from Death forever. People die everywhere, all over the place –nowhere's immune from death, I'm sure you can give me a million examples to prove that. So if nowhere's safe, there's nowhere to hide.'

'So, what, you're saying we should just confront Death?' mused Alexa, waving away an offer to simply have her head shaved.

'Exactly,' Robbie nodded, as he and Alexa swapped seats, the barber beaten into submission by the Ribiera locks. 'Why spend this time adopting a siege mentality?'

'Alright, let's say we do this whole 'look Death in the eye' job. What are we going to do, linger round hospitals or something?'

'No, I'm going to commit suicide.'

'Oh, come on, the movie's not that bad, is it?' joshed Alexa.

'Seriously,' insisted Robbie. 'There's nothing for me to look forward to, growing up in this backwoods town offers nothing. I'm already bored of it, already I'm wiped out and exhausted. If I can provide something worthwhile in death then it's a damn site more worthwhile than anything I ever achieved in life.'

Alexa frowned, turning back to the movie. 'You're being ridiculous. And melodramatic. It's very sweet to think that you could do it, that you died so I may live and all, but your death is not a fair trade for my life. I mean, you're still young. You've got years to make something of yourself. What makes you think it should end already?'

'I wanted to be an actor,' said Robbie. 'By my age, Jodie Foster, Drew Barrymore, Johnny Depp had all been in critically acclaimed movies. I can't get the lead role in school drama productions. I can't get extras roles in ITV dramas. The stuff I want to do, I can't.'

'Then learn your craft. You need the life experience, surely. Anyway, not all actors are precocious. Look at Bill Nighy, Ricky Tomlinson, er, that actress who plays all the grandmothers . . .'

'Look at Millie Kennedy. All her great work had been done by my age. And – and! –her mystique increased as a result of the 'tragic artist dies young' stuff.'

'Oh come on, don't you remember how this story ends?' Alexa turned back to Robbie, their eyes met. Robbie did not look as if he was interested in a discussion of the relative merits of the Millie Kennedy story.

Alexa frowned. 'Aren't there friends who can help? Or, you know, maybe you could go and see somebody about the way you're feeling.'

'What good would friends do?' said Robbie, suddenly angry. 'Just to spout some clichés that they've read or they've heard or they've watched in some crappy buddy cop movie? And counsellors, psychiatrists? They're no better: only difference there is, they've got training in recycling clichés from books and positive thinking manuals and all that shit, instead of movies and grunge albums.'

Alexa gave one of those nasal sighs which people do when stumped for an answer in a debate with a stubborn opponent. The problem was, Robbie was right. If Alexa had to pick the worst possible group to offer support to a terminal depressive with suicidal tendencies, teenage boys would only rank slightly lower than a herd of deaf-mute mountain goats. She didn't know a huge amount about the teenagers of today, outside of the lairy groups who bustled into the Bureau to stock up on Euros for a lads' weekend in Magaluf or Benidorm. Or maybe the groups who loitered on street corners and in bus stops drinking cider and wolf-whistling whose elder members' hormonal instincts Alexa had occasionally taken advantage of. Obviously she didn't go any younger than was strictly legal, of course: but from her experience, it was certainly true that a man's sexual peak was in his late teens and a woman's was around her sort of age, which was, um, older. However, she couldn't imagine that any of them would be able to provide much support in a time of need; most would be more likely to give an airy 'Shut up, you faggot' and rugby-tackle Robbie to the ground. Obviously that's a wild generalisation and a complete stereotype, but even if Robbie hung out exclusively with brooding, poetry-reading sensitive sorts from *Dead Poets' Society* or *The History Boys*, she wondered whether any of them would have the life experience and the articulacy to offer anything of use. Teenhood was strange: your emotions are all over the place and yet you're mocked by your peers if you show any of them.

A music mogul whose opinion of Millie Kennedy was second only to his opinion of himself boomed onto screen, curt ripostes rapidly cutting through Alexa's cluttered ruminations and bringing her into the present. She suppressed a smile. This was so obviously the wrong place for this discussion. You had this sort of conversation on the top of a tall building or something, not in a barbers' or in a cinema or in a combination of the two. Still, it made a change from 'Going anywhere nice on your holidays?'Come on Alexa, think. Say something.

'Hey, if it helps any, I'd be kinda pissed off if you went. I mean, we've only just met and all, but it seems to be going pretty well so far.'

'I'm serious Alexa. Whether or not I met you, I would end it all. The fact that this'll be the best chance of outrunning Death that we've got is a bonus – a bonus that we should use to our advantage. Do you have money?'

Alexa snorted. 'I didn't spend it *all* on booze and fags, y'know. Sure, I've got money.'

'Good. Because if I'm going to do this, I want to do it in a memorable way. I've got some ideas, but I'll need your help.'

Alexa paused. If, two days ago, she had been told that the life of a teenager she'd never met would be sacrificed to save her own, she'd happily accept it. But this was no anonymous teenager now, this was Robbie with his dishevelled hair, awkward nervous energy and self-hating intensity, who was willing to lay down his life for her own. It was the sort of heroic gesture that was typical of youth. A gesture that never looked likely to be carried out. For that reason, she had to accept: she could always talk Robbie out of it later. But then, what if she did talk him out of it? Would that mean that she'd end up sacrificing her own life for his? Was Robbie in even greater danger now just by way of association with her?

Alexa looked at Robbie, whose eyes were darting between the screen and Alexa, waiting on Alexa's next response. He'd been remarkably accepting of the whole situation. He didn't even know how she'd avoided death.

(IV)

I was in an underground opium den of the sort favoured in the Victorian era by the ilk of Mr Hyde and Dorian Gray and largely considered to have fallen into disuse at the end of the 19th century. Still, the greatest trick the Devil ever played was convincing the world that he didn't exist, and so it was with the opium dens, violently violating the smoking ban in London by producing more fumes than a diesel-powered Jeep. The den was accessible round the back of one of the Chinese novelty tat shops that you saw mysteriously appear in the high streets of

49

most cities. The sort which unfathomably stay open despite never selling anything of any value or indeed purpose. Of course I couldn't say that all of them are fronts for opium dens, but this one certainly was.

I'd been waiting for some time now for my acolyte Francisco to return with my newly-repaired magic carpet; an unreliable heap of junk which broke down constantly. Come to think of it, both the carpet and Francisco could be described as unreliable heaps of junk which broke down constantly. The carpet was allegedly my most reliable method of transport, which meant I was constantly resorting to train, raft or hot-air balloon to get anywhere. Francisco, meanwhile, had become pregnant during experiments with the opposite sex which don't need disclosing in the course of this tale. In any case, bad associates and good opium are a potent mix, and I was wondering whether to pass out, staring into the candlelight, when a shadowy figure approached through the smoke. As he approached, time appeared to freeze, although people becoming completely motionless were hardly unusual in this sort of establishment.

'Death, I'm guessing,' I coughed. 'You'll have to forgive me, I hadn't expected you so soon – if I had, I would have dressed up.'

'Save the crap, technomage,' snapped the newcomer.

'I see you've taken the Nine Inch Nails look,' I observed, 'another of those tedious cases of life imitating art, I think. I'm disappointed you don't have the scythe, but then I suppose that's the traditionalist in me coming out.'

'Listen, man, I didn't come here to discuss fashion, least of all with a guy who dresses like Merlin-'

'Hey, these clothes are practical AND comfortable, and anyway, I can't imagine Merlin wearing combat trousers!' The combats were a new addition to the robes, preventing up-robe breezes and providing a surprising amount of pocket space for alchemy, chemistry and clockwork explosives, all of which are essential for technomagic as I'm sure you're already aware.

'Alright, enough with the sartorial critique already. You're not lucky enough to meet Death, my name is Zan. I'm one of Death's, uh . . .*collectors*. These days, The Grim Reaper himself saves himself for the big ones – popes, kings, that kinda thing. He'll be there to do the whole grim reaping at the end of the world, but right now? There's too much dying for one immortal being. So that's where we come in: we collect the average guys of the world en route to their eternal afterlife, whatever *that* might be and . . . Are you even listening to me?'

I shook my head, attempting to clear some of the cobwebs out of it. 'Sorry, I'm feeling a bit spaced-out. Light-headed, maybe. I think it's the opium.'

'Actually no, it's a residual problem that comes with the heightened reality of being this close to death,' said Zan, matter-of-factly. 'The reason things seem so *unreal* to you is because this is the first time in your life that you're this close to something as inexorably and irrefutably real as death.

'Anyway, look, that's the explanation over with. Reason I'm here is, I had an appointment with a lady, Alexa Ribiera. She didn't show up.'

'Well, that's fascinating and I'm sorry to hear that you were stood up, but I hardly see how this applies to me.'

Whatever advantages the den has, it does not have the ability to conceal prevarication and alas, Zan saw through the smoke-addled subterfuge.

'Oh come on. The human race has been trying to cheat death since they first found out about it. Thousands of years later we've got somebody who's actually managed it, who's potentially going to achieve immortality and the only thing that's different now to thousands of years ago is not human cunning or ingenuity but technology. Combine technology with magic and you've got a combination which could both achieve the prevention of death and inadvertently bring about the end of the world as we know it. Now, funnily enough, when I think of technology and magic together, the word 'technomage' seems to fill both criteria, do you see what I'm getting at?'

'The end of the world?' I echoed, lagging behind somewhat (if you can be 'behind' when time has stopped).

Zan explained, although the exact words I don't remember and this segment has been dialogue-heavy already. In summation:

Death is as necessary a part of human life as birth and the endless cycle of renewal is crucial to the development of humanity. To not have death would mean eternal existence and to have that on a widespread, major level – which would be inevitable once it was discovered – would mean the stagnation of human progress. Not only that, but also overpopulation on an even grander scale. Economic crisis due to insufficient food, a society heavy on pensions and ultimate disaster for the planet as we know it today.

Imagine the effects in countries in which the corrupt dictator had declared himself leader for life, then managed to procure the secret of immortality. Assassination attempts would prove futile. Moreover, eternal life is not the same as eternal youth or eternal health, which would lead to a drain on the country's resources keeping the old tyrant alive. The continued existence of the dictator would have a potentially devastating impact on the country which would have to put up with proclamations and laws passed from an increasingly senile mind. The only way in which this could ever be resolved would be a risky coup or Iraq-style invasion which would potentially destroy foreign relations or destroy the country in a mass of uprisings and rebellion: the unnecessary deaths of many innocents due to the immortality of the guilty. It's heavy stuff indeed, which required a well-thought out follow-up with gravitas and depth. I paused for a while until I found something appropriate.

'What about zombies and vampires?'

'What?'

'Surely you know where the dead are likely to be due to an absence of their living. As if they're marked to die. Or you're able to monitor time and space, entering at the exact moment and exact co-ordinates that they're about to pass away. In that case can't you just check out where there's nothing where life should be? Like a zombie or a vampire?'

'They're totally different though – totally different. Zombies are living bodies without a soul. Vampires are souls without a living body. All we are interested in – have ever been interested in, or for that matter, able to track – is the exact moment when the soul is separated from the body. Right now with Alexa we've got a living soul in a living body, which makes it impossible to find in any way that we could use. What I need to know from you is how you did it and how we can catch her.'

Chapter Four

(I)

'You know, you could have just committed suicide on the Internet. At least we'd only have had to spend £15 on a webcam or something and we wouldn't have had to go traipsing around the world to do it.'

The suicide mission, Robbie had to concede, was not going well, mostly because he was still alive. It had all seemed so easy – he'd simply pick out one of his Top Ten Ways To Commit Suicide and run with it. However, the suicide methods had conspired to fail to the point where Robbie suddenly understood why so many people went for the blades 'n' pills combination – at least it was cheap and quick.

The thing was, as he had explained to Alexa, if he was never going to have achieved anything in his worthless teenage life, he may as well make his death something spectacular which people would talk about for years. Not in a Darwin Awards kinda way: he was too proud and too serious for that ignominious reputation. No, he wanted to go in a way that was remarkable, not remarkably stupid. That was the reason for the list! That was why his main hobby, his focal interest, was compiling weird stories and ideas from Bizarre, the National Enquirer and 'weird world' features and working out how they could be incorporated into his grand artistic project. That's why he had stayed up til 2am doing the Ten Places To Die. This said, it was a much better idea in theory than in practice, although suicide always is.

So they'd been to Gateshead early on, a nice easy jaunt, and found that the Angel of the North could not be used as a Wicker Man, which Robbie had previously been certain was the original intention of the sculpture. He'd considered a grandiose leap from a balcony seat at a performance of *Phantom of the Opera* only to find that he'd picked the one time of year where it was running in neither the West End nor in Broadway and no respectable performance was going on. In fact, a quick search suggested the biggest performance was in a state school in the middle of Suffolk and Robbie doubted there was going to be a balcony nor a shocked audience of hundreds. Such a death would be lucky to make the front page of the *Suffolking What* or whatever their local paper was called. Going further afield, they'd been to Vietnam where Robbie had planned to offer his life in place of the first sucker scheduled for the firing squad that day, only to find out, not surprisingly, that Vietnamese prisons were impenetrable fortresses. In any case, as Alexa pointed out on the way back to the boat, association with a paedophile or murderer was hardly a dignified exit.

They had been to a Civil War re-enactment in Gettysburg, in which Robbie's death, he hoped, would have the added bonus of having people question the inanity of what they were doing with their summers playing dress-up from hundreds of years ago. Alas, nobody was using real guns or cannons and you couldn't really throw yourself on a bayonet for fear of looking stupid. As if the shame would outlive him, or whatever that quote was. Besides, Robbie had to admit, the re-enactment guys turned out to be friendly and rootsy. All that they were doing, all things considered, was finding another way of passing a weekend in a way that served as

56

an excuse to get drunk with their mates while also celebrating their patriotism. It would seem wrong to ruin their day like that – it would be the equivalent of a drive-by at a jousting tournament.

The Argentinean football match, that was a rough one. Robbie had seen on TV somewhere that Argentine football was generally ruled over by mafia-style gangs and that the game was full of violence which turned fatal on a regular basis. The plan was to go to some fleabit lower league game or 0-0 midtable clash and invade the pitch, shout '¿podemos no todos apenas conseguira delante?' and promptly shoot himself. The Babelfish translation for 'Can't we all get along?' was a nice touch of attention to detail, Robbie thought. Unfortunately, this attention to detail did not spread to other aspects of the plan, for instance, where a gun would come from or which football match Alexa and Robbie should attend.

Eventually they headed to Buenos Aires hitching a ride with some radical left-wingers who discussed Che Guevara in broken English and how he had become just another face on a top from Primark and can you imagine Winston Churchill being reduced to that sort of status? They couldn't get tickets to the most important match that week, it being a fiercely contested local derby. Robbie didn't dare attempt to break into it in case of incarceration in an unforgiving South American jail: death had to *mean* something, otherwise it was irrelevant, and he didn't come to Argentina just to be beaten to death in jail while Alexa rotted in the same penitentiary indefinitely. So they spent their time in Buenos Aires having sex and visiting clubs that played awful techno in which Alexa had to talk Robbie out of punching a barman for asking what his mother was having. They did eventually get tickets to a match, which was cancelled dramatically when someone was shot whilst awaiting entrance to the stadium, rendering the match unplayable under the circumstances but, in Robbie's mind, also rendering his potential protest meaningless.

So the suicide attempts had not been successful and Robbie started to suspect that Alexa was becoming less than enthralled with the prospect of going to another country for another heroic failure at managing to die. If only he could make her understand that the whole reason for doing this was not some teenage ego thing but for her, to save her, the whole thing was and is and always will be about her.

(II)

There comes a point in your life where death is no longer something that happens to other people, but could happen to you at any point.

Maybe it's the point where you're watching your favourite sport and your team brings on its latest protégé and that protégé is no longer 'this guy' but 'this kid' and most of his teammates are younger than you, too. Maybe it's the point where your favourite songs to dance to when you go out stop being played at clubs. The point where you have to go to retro nights to dance nostalgically to songs that remind you of your first time high, or of the first time you went out underage and came home with no key at 2am and had to wake your parents up or sleep on the doorstep all night. Maybe it's the point where those memories become hazy and you can't remember what year they occurred in. Maybe it's the point where you don't know, don't care about, or worse, *don't understand* the music that's popular in the clubs or the charts these days. Maybe it's the point where all your friends have a wedding, a kid, a mortgage or all three, or the point where you really should seriously think about contributing to a pension or getting health insurance.

It's an almost imperceptible change. One morning, at some point between waking up after a refreshing night's sleep (no drinks last night, not when you have to be up early in the morning for work) and checking that you have your car keys, work pass and packed lunch, it might suddenly hit you that you're an adult. It might hit you that you haven't done anything you were aiming for and that the quiet of the grave is only tempting because at least you're going to get some peace, but it's coming closer and closer. What can you do? No wonder so many men have mid-life crises, get a motorbike and shack up with some harlot half their age.

Alexa wondered whether this was some sort of mid-life crisis. Certainly it fulfilled all the criteria – halfway across the world with a guy half her age after a broadly unremarkable life. A spectral existence which, looking back, seemed to have been one long plateau for the duration of her adult life. An existence in which the majority of the danger was lived vicariously through ultra-gory Japanese horror movies and through the sort of ultraviolent detective novels written by, and for, middle-aged women. Eventually and through repeated re-readings she realised that those middle-aged women enjoyed the books for the same reasons that she did: namely, that they dulled the monotony of her life.

Sometimes, particularly when she was younger, she'd attempted to spice her life up with random sexual encounters. Her backdrop of choice was a series of melancholy clubs where the floor was like glue, no doubt because it was broadly coated in the nefarious moonshine served to those who were prepared not to ask questions about its origin. For a while, these allegedly illegal places were illicitly thrilling but largely harmless and Alexa could relax in a place in which danger was at arm's length. Then, one day, the aggro that was normally scheduled in for 2am, which was always long after Alexa had left, was unexpectedly brought forwards and someone ended up going through a window. Suddenly the old fear was back and Alexa stopped going out.

Small wonder that she'd been so grateful to see Robbie or so easily seduced by his ostentatious scheme: it was danger, yes, but it was conducted for her own safety. If only her past self from as little as six months ago could see her now: travelling around the world, checking out all the places she'd only heard about, the places she'd always dreamed of going! It would seem unthinkable, implausible. Perhaps she'd even get on a plane next – or no, maybe that was a step too far, still, even now.

But there was a confidence to her now, much more so than before. Maybe this was because Death appeared to have been left behind in England. Maybe it was because there was no risk if there was zero possibility of death (although maybe there was still the possibility of injury? Alexa hadn't quite worked out how this works yet). Maybe it was because of Robbie and his impulsive recklessness making her feel invulnerable.

Or maybe she really had lost her mind. What a risk this had been for her, what a lot of trust she had had to invest in a teenager who she had only just met. Sure, she held the money and to that effect the power, but Robbie had the ideas, the direction. With Robbie, she felt safe walking through the nightlife of Argentina; without him there was a danger that all was lost and that Death was everywhere. Yet how well did she really know Robbie? What chance was there that he'd just vanish one day? How had she got here again?

(III)

Time is a much-misunderstood concept, not least by those who attempt to understand it in order to manipulate it. The idea that people can travel through time and change the world as it was a thousand years ago can be undermined by one simple observation: we haven't met any time travellers. If you went back to 1937 to assassinate Hitler, you'd fail, because we know that Hitler goes on to create pandemonium throughout Europe for the next eight years until he finally puts everyone out of their misery and commits suicide. You're not going back to some alternate version of 1937: it's the *same* 1937 as always, so the results are going to be the same.

However, just because you aren't able to kill Hitler in 1937 doesn't necessarily mean it's impossible to go back in time to 1937 and meet Hitler. It's just that if a time-traveller from the future was going to go into the past and kill anybody, we'd have found out by now. I mean, Hitler was probably shot at all the time, being a tyrannical oppressor of his own people and all that, and it's perfectly possible that a time traveller was one of the people who attempted to do so. But it didn't work, did it, because Hitler lived through 1937 and beyond into 1938, 1939 and World War Two. Of course, you'll say it's possible that a time traveller killed Hitler in 1945, or that it's possible that they prevented Hitler from being assassinated in the first place. It's possible, perhaps – but if I told you to go back in time to 1945 to kill Hitler, your first response would be 'well, he died in 1945 anyway, and that wasn't with the help of a time traveller,' so I'm pretty confident it didn't happen.

This said, providing all the elements are in place, it's possible to manipulate them to create a different result simply by moving the particles around, swapping the empty space for human particles and vice-versa. To go back to the Nazi example (and why not, I have British roots and the British are supposed to be obsessed by Nazis), you can't have an elephant fall on Hitler's head midway through a rally, but you could have an elephant trample on him midway through a mundane visit to the zoo. Assuming, that is, that this visit was recorded.

I discovered this technology while running CCTV footage through a VCR connected to a digital TV box one night, one of those Sky+ jobs which allow you to pause, rewind and fast-forward through television programs although unfortunately only TV programs you've already recorded. You wonder how much more interesting, say, the National Lottery would be if you skipped through all the chat and straight to the draw, not to mention advantageous to gambling. Sport, too: you could skim through a match to see whether you were in for a thriller or another dreary England collapse. I attempted it with a

Test match I'd recorded over the course of a few days and even in quadruple speed the action failed to become exciting.

But I digress. I was watching the CCTV footage – the reasons for and details behind its accrual are unnecessary here – on a VCR while simultaneously meddling with a video manipulation package that I'd acquired on a laptop called the Technonomicon. The Technonomicon, which was becoming a liability already, had been I'd acquired from a mysterious backstreet technology vendor who I'd travelled to meet in California, who was hawking knocked-off junk from the Googleplex. Apparently, like all major organisations concerned with the ruling of the world, Google had been meddling in the dark arts and found a whole variety of technological ghosts and ghoulies that, terrified, they promptly sold on the black market. The salesman warned me that the Technonomicon was possessed by black magic and had a mind of its own, but I wasn't particularly bothered; in my experience, that fits the description of most computers.

That particular night, I undertook a gruelling 48-hour blaze of creativity in which samosas, chai and a vile but agreeably intoxicating cocktail of Kahlua and Raki (any magician will experiment with combining the potions in his laboratory and apply the same discipline to combining all the booze in his cupboard: the results of both are potentially disastrous) acted as my only sustenance. Revelations and masterful breakthroughs came in a flurry unexpected by even the most brilliant technomage i.e. myself. Firstly, I discovered that I could organise remote viewing of the CCTV footage onto my laptop: I realise you're underwhelmed by this mundane satellite system, but stick with me. I then found that I could run it through the mysterious Google black magic video manipulation program and, given that the footage was live, I could copy and paste things around the room for my own amusement. It wasn't especially interesting to begin with: the room was dark and unoccupied, and after a few hours, I began to wonder whether I was hallucinating, particularly given that when I reached for my food or booze, it constantly seemed to be in a different place to where I'd put it. However, when a security guard came in to check the room and nearly fell over an umbrella tree that I'd placed in the doorway for amusement, I realised that I could manipulate space remotely.

I may be a magician and a technologist *par extraordinaire* but one of the things I've become most acutely aware of in my travels around the world is that slapstick is funny whoever you are, so an unsuspecting uniform going arse-over-tit appealed to me enough to hit the rewind button and watch again. So I did, a couple of times, in fact, while sipping another RaKahlua and nearly throwing up, until drunkenness got the better of me and I hit the fast-forward button instead of the rewind button. Another revelation: I could see into the future. But was the future read-only, or could I . . ? I moved a sign to another wall, then hit 'rewind' to get me back up to date with the present. The sign was back on its original wall. An hour later, it moved over. I felt pleased with the discovery, but merely toying with the interior decoration of a bank was boring. I fast-forwarded through a month or two, trying to see whether there was anything interesting going on.

Eventually I discovered a shoot-out in what appeared to be a bungled raid at the bank in which the lady I would later know to be Alexa Ribiera was shot by one of the criminals, who was obviously panicking that the heist was not going according to plan.

The vision haunted me. Seeing death was never pleasant, but seeing a death that hadn't even happened, yet was inevitably going to happen, was even worse. Of course, I could simply report it to the police or the bank, ensuring that they took sufficient precautions to prevent the shoot-out happening at all: but here you run the risk of being accused of collaboration or worse, instigation; and that's assuming that you're believed in the first place. Plus, aside from a sentimental attachment formed through hours of watching their CCTV footage, I didn't have much empathy for a bank losing a bunch of money. A person losing their life: now you're talking.

I resolved to help Alexa, although of course there was a condition: technomages don't live on air, shady discarded technology, shamanic potions and shifty narcotics have to come from somewhere and I was running out of all three. I decided to embark on the sort of public duty which would also involve my making a tidy profit, although of course I had to initially embark on the sort of research which could also involve my being arrested for stalking.

Eventually I found Alexa using some more technomancy, a form of reverse image-search in which copying and pasting her image into a search engine resulted in a number of matches for her in her capacity as bureau du change agent.

Naturally I considered what would be the most appropriate and sensitive way of handling this curious and delicate subject. Unfortunately, still reeling from the lack of sleep and the inebriating toxic brew, I decided that the best way would be to rush up to her after she'd finished work, shouting 'YOU'RE GOING TO DIE!' and waving the evidence, printed from the diabolic laptop, in her face. Amazingly, I'd correctly guessed her fear of death, which was even more pronounced in Alexa than even the rest of the mortality-obsessed human race, for reasons which would later become clearer to me. But at that point, I couldn't have cared less about her past; all that was important was her future, as in, the continuation of same, and her wallet, as in, the opening of same.

Having accrued the generous up-front commission that was required to continue my research, I had to consider carefully what the best way of manipulating the video was going to be. I couldn't swap the gun for, say, a pen: the bullet was still going to be fired at force. This simple physics also negated swapping the bullet and pen. A pen travelling at the same velocity the bullet was being fired would have harpooned Alexa anyway. We couldn't merely reposition the shooter: you'd run the risk of somebody else dying unnecessarily. Deleting Alexa from the picture was impossible: the program closed down on half the attempts to do it and on the other half, simply refused. In any case, deleting her would have been ridiculous: multiple witnesses and several cameras would testify to the fact that Alexa had just vanished into thin air, which would lead to questions and more unnecessary publicity. I had no interest in saving Alexa's life only to end up having the rest of that life spent through the mire of television, radio and newspaper hackos pestering her every day.

Of course, Alexa could simply stay at home instead of going to pay in that cheque or whatever on Earth she was doing. But I didn't think that that would work either: the future is as intransient as the past and whatever Alexa attempted to do that day, she'd somehow have ended up in that bank for some wildly implausible reason. The evidence was in black and white: she would be there.

Eventually I realised I could just copy and paste Alexa eight inches to the right and avoid the bullet entirely, which proceeded to tragically end the life of the hapless umbrella tree. Although I didn't know it until Zan proceeded to pester me while I was celebrating my success by spending its profits, I had created immortality.

Chapter Five

(I)

Waking up with a gun held against your head is never a pleasant experience, but when it's your loved ones holding the gun, it's even worse.

'I should just end it now,' hissed Alexa, who was stood over Robbie, holding the gun to his temple. 'Before this mission kills us both.'

'What are you on about?' Robbie managed. Like most teenagers he was no good in the mornings to start with and now he was expected to have a clear conversation at gunpoint. 'Of course it will kill us both.'

'What kind of suicide are you? Most kids who want to kill themselves do it with a shoelace tied to their ceiling or with a razorblade or something. Not this, not a journey halfway around the goddamn world for some novelty killing.'

Robbie had a fleeting muse on whether there was such a thing as hangover psychosis, but dismissed it. 'What can I say? It's my life's work.'

A flicker of a smile ghosted over Alexa's face, but she continued. 'It's insane, is what it is. End it here and now and we both get what we need. You die, Death turns up and we fight there.'

Robbie chanced his luck. 'You'll never do it.'

'Try me.'

'You'll never do it, you'll never become one of the stars of those chicklit police procedurals you read.'

Alexa cocked the trigger. 'What do I have to lose? I'm already dead. You want to die. Seems like a mutually beneficial arrangement to me.'

Robbie shrugged. 'Why not? 'British tourists dead, locals baffled' – I can see the headlines on the Sun and the Star now. There is one problem, though.'

'Which is?'

'You don't know what the hell you're doing.' Robbie sat up, Alexa keeping the gun to his head. 'How do you know that you won't just end up blowing my face off, or leaving me brain-damaged? What happens if I don't die? As soon as that gun goes off we'll have people up here ready to put you in jail. This is the sort of country where you'll get a sentence for like 834 years and if you're immortal, that's a sentence you'll end up carrying out. And what will you be thinking of throughout that time? Nothing but the blood, the fragments of the bone, the pain, the anguish.'

Alexa's arm dropped. She loosened her grip on the gun. At the same time, Robbie reached up and snatched the gun from her hands. Jumping up, Robbie reversed the situation and held the gun to Alexa's head.

'On the other hand,' Robbie resumed, 'a murder is punishable by death here. What do either of us have to lose in that situation? You're already dead and I'm a suicide wannabe. I could just sentence you to meet your maker right now without having to worry about challenging Death myself. I'd be famous, you'd be dead and the universe would be how it's supposed to be. Not how it *should* be, but how it's meant to be.'

'You wouldn't.'

'Why not?'

'Because as soon as the gun goes off we'll have half the building up here. The police won't be too far away. Then the journalists. Do you really want the photo that the world sees to be a picture of you in nothing but grey boxers?'

Robbie looked down. Alexa was right – no murderer with any credibility would dress like this. He opened the chamber of the gun and emptied it, went over to the window, opened it, and threw both the bullets and the gun out of the window. He looked back at Alexa and gave a crooked smile.

'I don't think either of us have the capacity for murder, do we?'

'It was looking close for a moment there, though,' murmured Alexa distantly.

'Sorry. Things got intense there for a moment.'

'Yeah, but let's not do a post-mortem when nobody's dead,' shrugged Alexa, lighting up a cigarette. I just . . . this is all weird and unusual to me, I don't know if I'm entirely comfortable doing it anymore.'

Robbie sat down next to her on the bed. 'I think maybe I should try and find some ways of carrying this off which don't put you in mortal danger just getting there. Luckily, I've got some ideas. I think it eliminates the bungee-jump/Zorb idea though.'

'What bungee-jump/Zorb idea?'

'Never mind.'

'So tell me about your friends,' Alexa asked suddenly. They'd been waiting to go up for an hour and a half now, and tempers were starting to fray a little.

'What about them?' asked Robbie.

Alexa shrugged. 'I don't know, I just wanna know who you hang out with, I suppose.'

'Uh, well, they're different from me I guess. They're into, like, science and sport. Stuff that I'm not particularly interested in. It's weird, we used to be close but . . .' He trailed off.

'But what, you developed different interests and different personalities? Found out that just being in the same school wasn't enough to maintain a friendship? Drifted apart a bit once you realised that none of you were into the Cabbage Patch Kids anymore?'

'Into the what?'

'It doesn't matter. But am I right?'

'About everything except the cabbage kids,' Robbie nodded. Alexa was right. It was weird how much stuff she was right about with him.

'It happens, Rob. People move on, it's inevitable that you'll grow apart, particularly in school, you know? Anyway, having different interests doesn't necessarily mean you can't be friends?'

Robbie wasn't convinced. Yeah, people had different interests to each other, but it seemed as if people's interests were largely tolerated or at least ignored, but not his. Robbie remembered trying to read some of the poetry he use to write to his friends, which led to derision for weeks. Realising it wasn't for him, Robbie drifted into acting: at least that way led to his delivering great lines which people would take seriously and more importantly, weren't written by him. If the lines he was saying were execrable, at least he hadn't written them, he'd just be working with the material he was given. Also, easier to be famous. Anyway, Robbie's friends, he had decided, were jerks.

'What were your schooldays like?'

'Um, different. They were that long ago, they were in black and white. Surely you've got acting friends?'

Alexa lit a cigarette. Robbie suspected Alexa was changing the subject deliberately here but decided to leave it for fear of rocking the boat with her. Anyway, 'acting friends'? People pretending to be friends? Most of his friends seemed to be like that anyway. Oh wait, she meant 'actor friends'.

'I don't think you have friends in acting if you're in competition for the same roles. There's people I get on with, I guess, but they're a bit . . . pretentious I suppose. A bit melodramatic, a bit self-serious. They're all in plays because their parents are fucking pushy about it and they're prepared to kiss the fucking arse of the casting agent.'

'Casting agent?'

'Well, drama teacher, you know what I mean. The kids at school who want to act are . . . look, in a school's drama group you've got camp kids and wusses and all the school's really interested in is getting two attractive kids centre-stage so that, when they put on their shows, they can say "Look what great, handsome, well-adjusted, totally heterosexual kids we've got coming out of this school!" If the kids have parents who are insisting they go in that direction then so much the better for the school, y'know? You don't want someone with messy hair and a big nose to take the lead.'

Alexa smiled. 'You don't have a big nose, it's, I dunno, distinguished maybe. What's all this about pushy parents anyway? You mean yours aren't?'

Robbie shook his head. He was in the middle of South America with a woman he barely knew and yet he was hardly seeing his photo on milk cartons. His parents wouldn't notice he was gone, most likely.

'What are your family like?'

'Gone,' Alexa said dismissively, then, 'Hey, looks like we're ready to go!'

(III)

Another wasted exploration of the town Alexa Ribiera had been living in for most of her time and Zan was getting irritated. He'd fast-forwarded a bit, stepping into a point two weeks later than her disappearance and found nothing. He'd attempted to explore a bit, but it was tricky: the physical world existed on a different metaphysical plane to the one that he did and therefore the only things he could really see were dead and awaiting collection. Looking out of a window he saw The Death Of Cats rounding up various rodent corpses and chasing them off to the afterlife – nobody enjoyed their job more than the fat tabby cat who went under the pretentious (and misleading) name The Death Of Cats. Otherwise, it was like looking for your car keys in the middle of a power cut where you couldn't find a torch or a candle.

It wasn't always this difficult. As Alessandro Bonetti, he had, in his physical life, been a fine hunter, working initially under the Mafia, who paid him to root out people who had crossed them. He hadn't gone in for killing or torture when rounding up victims for the Mafia, partially for his own safety as he didn't wish to spoil the Mafia's fun, but partially because he realised that he wasn't into it. Later, when arrested for the same, he served a few years inside for aiding and abetting crime and was encouraged by the screws to go straight and work on their side, where he worked under mostly the same principles except without all the killing. He had to use more unorthodox, unscrupulous methods to catch these guys, which meant that the reports handed in by police officers served as creative writing half the time. Despite this, or perhaps because of it, he was good at his job and whilst he didn't exactly reduce crime in the city, at least he maintained it at roughly the same level.

He had died on the job, inevitably: he raided a house in which the occupant was wanted for armed robbery and caught the assailant in his flat, where he had just created a Molotov cocktail, ready to kill himself and everyone who went with him. Zan knew that, given the angle of his arm, the villain was planning to throw it in Zan's general direction rather than his own. He waited for the throw, then ran for his enemy, effectively shoulder-tackling him out of the window, where they both toppled out as the home-made bomb exploded.

It was a straight fall: one floor, and Zan had done this enough to avoid serious injury: a broken rib or two, maybe. His opponent absorbed most of his weight and

Zan's too, though, and was struggling for breath, but Zan couldn't care less, distracted by the flames and the sudden shouts of kids from a ground floor flat directly below the one he'd just jumped out of.

'Ah crap,' muttered Zan, running to the window and smashing it with his elbow. The glass created a wound that was probably ugly and started to bleed, but Zan had no time to worry about that. He climbed in through the window.

Smoke was everywhere, and staring through the smog, coughing, he saw that some of the roof was caving in, presumably because of the impact of the bomb combined, no doubt, with the rising damp and piss-poor structures of this kind of building. Behind that were the children, both under eight, with a guardian nowhere to be seen.

Zan ducked the crumbling masonry, picked up the kids and rushed to the window, lifting them through the smoke and out to safety, one after the other, as carefully as possible. Zan climbed up himself, then slipped on the windowsill and landed on the broken glass, a shard going through his thigh. The pain was agonising, his leg useless. Still, he reached up, attempting to crawl through the window, and at that moment the entire ceiling caved in and Alessandro Bonetti was no more.

The hot air balloon drifted casually upwards, toying with gravity, letting itself get dragged down by it, letting gravity think that it had won for a while, then suddenly revealing that it was smarter and stronger and escaping land. Exhilarated, it gave a roar acting as a laugh to gravity, which shook its fist uselessly from the ground.

Alexa revealed a hitherto undisclosed bottle of Brazilian wine and started to uncork it, waving away the protestations of the pilot who, in any case, was protesting in Portuguese, a language Alexa couldn't speak. Despite her exotic name, the Latin-American roots of the Ribiera family were betrayed more than three generations back and Alexa had a tin ear for language.

'No hablo, er, Portugesie,' Alexa dismissed and at that moment, the balloon lurched awkwardly, leaving the pilot to attend to ballooning matters while continuing to make vile insults to the ignorant English.

Meanwhile, having found nothing at the Ribiera household, then, Zan returned to Limbo, thinking that he really ought to do some work other than the Alexa Ribiera thing for a bit: it's not as if there wasn't anything to do. That was the problem with being a banshee: there was never any down time.

As he gathered the plague wagon for another collection, he was stopped by the Angel Gabriel.

'Uh-oh, the Messenger of God, this doesn't bode well,' groaned Zan, although he was only messing around with

Gabe. Zan liked talking to Gabriel, mostly because he always had new stuff to report, while Gabriel was envious of Zan getting to go down to Earth so many times (or so he claimed: in reality, the idea of someone so close to God displaying one of the deadly sins was unlikely). On Earth, Gabriel was best known for meeting the Virgin Mary and Muhammad and still acted as God's messenger in various capacities. However, he was also involved in running the prayer call centre at the centre of the Earth, in which prayers were sifted for their content and those containing the Seven Deadly Sins or violating the Ten Commandments were rejected. Not many made it through the net, unsurprisingly. Sometimes Zan wondered how Gabriel found the time, and had to remind himself that time was non-existent here.

'It's just a bit of gossip from the prayer centre, Zan, nothing to worry about too much,' whispered Gabriel. 'I thought it may be of interest to you – it's a prayer we picked up from someone in South America.'

'Well, it sounds thrilling so far Gabe, carry on.'

'It says this: *please don't let Death catch Alexa tonight.* Any idea what that would be about?'

Zan froze in his tracks – in any other setting, 'stopped dead' would be the phrase. He attempted nonchalance. 'Well, language is pretty ambiguous, Gabriel. Doesn't your autobiography teach you that? All that nonsense about 'through a mirror darkly' and all that other stuff that left itself wide open to mistranslation and misuse?'

'This isn't just a case of mistranslation, Zan,' reproached Gabriel. 'We can translate every language, we'd be a bit of a useless centre if we couldn't. That's why I'm talking to you in English rather than Aramaic, Greek, Hebrew or any other language I could talk to you in. And speaking of English, that's the language that this prayer came to us in. This isn't some sort of kids' prayer or worries about ghosts and ghoulies- it quite clearly states 'catch' rather than 'come for' or anything else that would make sense. Rather than going straight to old Azrael himself, I figured I'd see if it meant anything to you lot.'

'Yeah, definitely for the best that, Gabe,' said Zan, affecting a nonchalant air while reaching for the card. 'No need to go bothering Him Indoors if it's not desperately urgent, right? Who sent the prayer?'

'This guy, Robbie Adams. At the time of this prayer, he was seventeen. No real consistent history of prayer . . .'

'And the date of this particular prayer is-' Zan broke off. 'Thanks for this, Gabriel, you mind if I keep hold of it? I might have a word with Azrael myself, but don't you worry about it. I'll see you later, yeah? Well, not *later* but, well, y'know.'

Gabriel made to reply, but the death chariot was already gone and at that same moment the balloon escaped the trees and started to soar above the rainforest.

'You know, I know I probably said this about all the other alternatives we've explored before, but this one really is perfect,' Robbie was saying.

'Uh-huh,' said Alexa, swigging the wine as the balloon continued to rise.

Robbie took the bottle. 'No, I mean it this time. I mean, it's straightforward and it shouldn't put you in any risk. I fall, Death turns up, I challenge him, you fly to safety.'

Alexa looked into his eyes. 'Do you have any idea what you'll do when you see Death?'

'Of course not. I think that's half the fun.'

78

'Are you scared?'
'Only a lot.'

Zan cruised the plague wagon into the middle of the rainforest. Man, there was so much *life* here, it was distracting. There was shit under his feet, crawling up the trees, flying above – even this river was full of life, not like those British ones full of pollution, shopping carts and nuclear waste but no fish. If he remembered right, Quetzalcoatl still did the Brazil gig. It was a depressing experience, from what he'd heard. Escorting people to their death is never going to be a barrel of laughs, granted, but there was so much child death in the South American countries, man, there were kids in the slums dying every day.

Zan didn't have much time here. By his reckoning it was 12.50 now. There were strict rules of space-time which related directly to the death collectors. To make sure that they weren't endlessly entering the same parts of history, only one of them could occupy a particular point in space-time and there was no chance of re-entry. No spiritual or physical body could occupy the same space in space-time more than once either, so you couldn't meet your past or future self and you certainly couldn't rectify the screw-ups you'd made. Zan had heard about quantum physics and how at a subatomic level electrons *could* occupy the same space at two points simultaneously, but as far as he understood it, a spiritual body was not sub-atomic. Anyway, Quetzalcoatl had sealed off every point up until now, and returned to the forest at 12.55, giving Zan five minutes.

The balloon had reached a steady height now. Robbie looked down. Was he imagining it or did the real world suddenly seem . . . imaginary? Irrelevant? The air was thinner all of a sudden, probably due to the altitude, but it was making him dizzy. The only thing that seemed truly real was the forest, lurking below him, ready to welcome him to oblivion. The heart of darkness, Robbie thought, was waiting for him.

Zan looked up. Existing on a different astral plane meant that the 'real' world was kind of murky to him, but he could make something out above him. A plane?

Robbie took one final swig of the wine and handed it back to Alexa. 'This is it, you know.' They hugged. 'I just want to say thanks. It's been good. Really.' Robbie turned to climb out of the balloon.

It was a balloon, Zan realised, and he found himself wondering whether his cargo was waiting for him there.
'Wait.'
It was 12.52. Zan figured that rather than stopping time and collecting his bounty, he could allow time to run, see what happened here. He was probably over-using the time-stopping spell anyway, he had a creeping feeling that somewhere it was being audited and he'd find himself having to explain what he'd been doing.

'What do you mean, wait?'

'Look at this stuff, Robbie.'

Robbie looked again. There was the rainforest, the Amazon, there were the river people whose entire life revolved around the river, living in tree houses and walking on rope bridges because the ground was flooded. There were exotic birds, lizards, insects, you could hear it in the air even if you couldn't make them out across the trees and probably, somewhere, there lurked some horrible South American carnivorous animals waiting to eat him. There were whole groups of people, Robbie had read, who had never been discovered by explorers and who had never wanted to be who were living somewhere in that forest. They'd only been seen by helicopter. Man, the place was alive alright.

Zan wondered whether he was infringing on Quetzalcoatl's territory just by being here. This was important, though.

'Why don't you stay for the ride?'

'What?!'

12.53. Man, this was drawn out. Alexa probably wasn't even in that hot air balloon. He didn't have any evidence for it, after all.

'Just have one memory of how glorious it is to be alive, Robbie! Think of it: you're in beautiful surroundings, the sun is out, we've got a decent mid-range wine here and you're with . . . well, you're in good company anyway. Let's keep going. You can commit suicide anytime you want, but let's have this one memory of our time together where we're actually doing something like a proper couple and not trying to avoid being shot or to pretend we're in the Civil War.'

12.54. It dawned on Zan that he could just enter the hot air balloon, not being bound by any of the constrictions of the physical world.

Robbie paused. It was beautiful alright.

The air blurred as if no longer important. Zan manifested in the air behind them.

Robbie smiled. 'Let's do it.'

Zan had not calculated properly. He was about ten feet away from the balloon. Luckily gravity was irrelevant to him in his non-physical state so he would avoid a Wile E Coyote plunge into the depths below, so he could just catch up. He ran after the balloon, but it was moving too quickly and Zan realised that even released from physical constraints, he could not catch it up. Shit, he'd blown it again. Why the hell hadn't he stopped time before he came here? He'd been so complacent, so fucking arrogant. The thought kept him company as he ran out of time and vanished from Earth.

12.55. The balloon sailed on.

Chapter Six

(I)

Alexa and Robbie were on a boat heading towards the group of islands variously called Oceania and Australasia in the company of Club 1830, a historical re-enactment holiday club for steampunks which involved investigating events and areas of historical curiosity in a twee fashion.

'Only last year,' their ringleader and founder member Annie-Key Walker had explained, as they looked over the side, Alexa chain-smoking, back turned to avoid seeing the sea and thinking of drowning, of icebergs and of killer whales, 'we visited Mount Tambora in Indonesia, which was responsible for 1816, the year without a summer. You know that it was indirectly responsible for the writing of Frankenstein AND the formation of the Church of the Latter-Day Saints?'

'So it created a famous monster known throughout the world AND Frankenstein?' asked Alexa, dryly.

Their next location coincided with one of Robbie's interests. However, given Alexa's allergy to flying (despite having cheated death and having flown in a hot-air balloon, she still worried about flying by plane, as if the air stewardess was going to pull out a scythe at any moment), sea travel was the only realistic way forward. As a result, they found themselves making conversation with Annie-Key and her group during the many-day ferry journey.

'You're pretty straight for someone called Annie-Key,' Robbie wondered aloud. He was right: Annie-Key Walker was a studious-looking young woman with a sensible haircut, despite her esoteric profession and interest: Club 1830 had gone from being an interest at university for slightly nerdy history buffs to something which was, if not a blowaway success, at least enough to sustain Annie-Key as a regular full-time job.

Annie-Key smiled, drawing on a menthol cigarette. 'Time was, I was a rebellious teenager just like you. The problem is how to be rebellious when your parents are radical anarchists. How can you stay out til 3am drinking and getting tattoos if your parents are going to come home at 4am, more drunk and with more tattoos? It didn't take that long to realise that the things that they despised were the obvious things to become interested in. So I got interested in history – they were all about the future. I started dressing plainly while they were in leather and piercings and tattoos.'

'I don't understand why you'd rebel against your parents, really,' Alexa mused. Oblivious to the looks that Robbie and Annie-Key gave her, she pressed on: 'When I was a kid, my dad was still way into the whole teddy-boy thing. He rolled up in a Cadillac, quiff and denim jacket, and dropped me and my brother off to school. The kids at my school, they used to laugh their arses off, but fuck them. I was never going to be like them, never wanted to be, so *my* rebellion was to worship the 1950s like my dad did, to listen to Bill Haley, to watch *Rebel Without A Cause* ten times a week and to dress like some waitress in a hot-dog bar. I suppose back then, I just liked the attention, I wanted to stand out and if that meant that girls were bullying me then I had to learn to bully back. Anyway, can we go in now? This cigarette's been completely ruined by all the sea air getting into my lungs.'

Robbie couldn't remember hearing a longer speech from Alexa. As they walked back below deck, he took Alexa's hand. 'You know, you've never talked about your past.'

'You've never asked.'

'Yeah, but I've told you about my family, y'know? You didn't have to ask about that. I don't know anything about your family, anything you've done really. It's like before you didn't die, you didn't live.'

'Yeah, yeah you've told me about your family, the family who probably don't even know you've gone.'

'My family couldn't give a shit whether I'm there or not anyway, what makes you think it'll be any different now? They won't even notice – I mean, you don't even know my family!'

'Look, they'll have noticed, OK? Christ, you lose a family member and you notice, alright, you notice every *fucking* day. You know why I don't talk about my past? Because some stuff's too painful to talk about. Some stuff, you don't need to know about. I'm going to our cabin, I mean, we do HAVE a cabin don't we? We're not just sleeping in the engine or something like the way your plans normally turn out?'

'Well yeah, we've got a cabin, all our stuff's there,' replied Robbie, bewildered by the direction the conversation had suddenly taken.

'Fine, listen, I'm going back there, I'll see you later' and with that Alexa stormed off into the midst of the ferry.

'Alexa . . . I'm . . . sorry?' guessed Robbie, but to no avail. Robbie was despondent: if he was going to kill himself, he might as well spend the time before that with someone whose company he enjoyed, and he enjoyed Alexa's. He liked Alexa, in fact you could even say that . . . But anyway, fuck her. The whole reason he was doing any of this was so that he could finally meet up with the Grim Reaper and talk him out of taking Alexa, not for himself. Although okay, the suicide would be pretty cool. But how many other guys would kill themselves for their girlfriend's benefit? We're talking about a huge romantic gesture here, goddamnit.

(II)

Alexa is seven on a misty day, shifting from foot to foot and waiting for her mother to get on the plane already.

All this had become pretty routine over the last year or so, her mother jetting away on some highly-paid international business conferences every month or two, leaving Alexa and her brother with her father. Her father who right now is wondering whether he should have put more money in the Pay and Display machine so that the Caddy doesn't get clamped.

'Now I know you're pretty bummed that Mummy isn't here to see your display, Alexa. Trust me, you'll thank me when you're older.' Alexa would wonder, years later, why she'd said something as banal as that; no doubt it was like one of those disclaimers you see on television before a clip of someone sawing their head off for magic: 'The following is done for your own good, so please don't discuss this on the psychiatrist's couch in fifteen years' time.'

'I just wanted you to see this one. It's important.'

'Oh, Alexa, I'm sorry I haven't been around much. I promise I'll make it up to you. Once this conference is done I should be home more, then we can spend lots more time together, okay?'

More trite banalities. When you're a kid you don't have time to sit around thinking how much better it would be if your mum wasn't working 80-hour weeks or if your dad played board games more often and watched the rugby and snooker less, you just get on with it. Who really cares which adults are in the room paying taxes and drinking beer when there is ballet and dolls and dancing and reading and horses? To go jetting off on some boring work thing when there's performance to be watched though, that's different. The world revolves around you when you're a kid. Perhaps it always does. The idea that there's something more important than watching you doing 30 seconds of ballet with ten other indistinguishable brats in between some interminable performances from the rest of the junior school is unthinkable. It didn't matter whether Ribiera Snr was there or not most of the time, but this was just one time, and she couldn't even manage that. That's why Alexa is sulking.

Her mother kisses her, her brother and her father goodbye and takes the walk to the plane, while the other Ribieras get back into their Cadillac, mercifully not clamped, and speed down the motorway back home, with the intention of getting some lunch and some smart clothes before going out to see Alexa's performance. Donny gripes about having to go but it's tough, there's no babysitter and Donny would expect Alexa to see his play at Christmas right? Right. So we're going.

Alexa never makes it that night. They're halfway ready when there's a knock on the door from the police. The night was foggy, the plane her mother was on couldn't land properly and crashed some 30 miles from the airport. Eleven deaths, one of which was Milana Ribiera.

Alexa never dances again.

(III)

Alexa recaps this to Robbie, having patched it up with him an hour earlier, in a bar on the boat which serves a variety of hot snacks and plays a Millie Kennedy CD. The snacks and the CD share the same consistently bland and ignorable qualities; but then, with Kennedy, this is little different from the majority of her output.

'I know you're frustrated at your acting going nowhere, I know how you feel. Up until that point, I had a similar dream. When I was seven I imagined thrilling audiences in opera houses, performing in front of kings, in front of Russian royalty, all that sort of thing. Dreadful nonsense, obviously: I'd watched *The Red Shoes* one too many times I think.'

She lit a cigarette, not knowing whether it was permitted and not caring either, providing that the barman didn't catch them (even then, he could hardly throw them overboard). 'Most people at least get to adulthood before their dreams are crushed – mine died that night. I couldn't possibly dance again when every time I did, it reminded me of that. Couldn't fly, couldn't get close: everything that involved risk I thought of what could happen. I mean, my mum could die on a routine business visit to Switzerland: it wasn't as if she was landing in, I dunno, Rwanda. That meant anything was possible, anything potentially dangerous. So that's why we're not on a plane at the moment watching some third-rate family comedy and cutting a day and a half out of our journey. I can't fly, y'know?'

'So what about the rest of your family?' Robbie asked. 'I mean, you had a brother and a father, they were there for you, right?'

Alexa sighed. 'Yeah they were – and for a while they were a comfort, until Donny and I started to realise that we were taking care of more and more of Mum's old responsibilities around the house. Dad had started to drink. It's one of those things you don't really notice when you're a kid and he'd already given us the whole thing about all of us needing to pull together and work harder and all that, but I mean, he wasn't feeding us and he wouldn't eat himself, it's just simple things like that.'

She smiled, half to herself. 'I mean, all teenagers are embarrassed by their parents and when you've got him turning up with his quiff and his Cadillac, it's even worse. But he had nobody else, and neither did we. What else could we do? We'd always defend him against the other kids, but when he's turning up drunk . . . you're fighting a losing battle, you know?'

Alexa paused for so long that Robbie wasn't sure that she hadn't finished. On the other hand, Robbie suspected she had more to say and in any case, he was out of his depth with this conversation.

'Most of the last couple of years Donny and I were living at home I think Dad was just waiting for us to move out so that he could start his mid-life crisis. About six months after I moved out, he bought a motorcycle. Six months after that he went out on his bike after about a half-bottle of whisky and wrapped it around a tree.'

She waved her cigarette in Robbie's general direction. 'So I guess I learnt to live in fear. The drinking and the smoking I do is kinda different. Nobody dies from being drunk. What you die from is getting behind the wheel of a car, or getting drunk and taking your motorbike out, or deciding to jump off a bridge because it 'seems fun'. What you die from is not being responsible about your own actions when you're drunk, okay. I've never seen anyone die as a direct result of having a drink or a smoke. But I have seen someone die from getting on a plane and I know from reading about them about plenty of people who've died from all sorts of other crazy shit.

'But why wouldn't I be scared of that? You know, why should I want to embrace life when it's given me nothing? Before you came along I was alone, pretty much. Why wouldn't I want to rail against death? Why wouldn't I want to defy it? Why is it fair that it's taken so much from me, but that it still isn't satisfied? Why should it take me as well?'

Robbie frowned. 'You say you're alone. I know it must have been tough on you losing both your parents. But there's Donny, right?'

Alexa smiled mirthlessly. 'Sure, there was Donny. Yeah, for a while we were tight. Then after Dad died, he went travelling and it was while he was in China that he . . .' She trailed off, extinguished her cigarette and ran her hand through her hair.

90

'It's alright Alexa,' Robbie said in what he hoped was a reassuring tone, and took the hand which was not still repeatedly stubbing her cigarette butt against the table. It was easy to do emotion when you were acting it out for the seventeenth row to see, but when it came to expressing real emotions in an intimate setting, he was still awkward and hopelessly lacking in experience.

'He'd been told before he went away that he was ill, but he ignored it, he'd been saving up for months and all the flights were booked... then he wouldn't look after himself properly would he? And I know I'm being stupid blaming the travel for it but that's how I felt, that another member of my family had gone away and the same result.. . Then every time anyone came in to buy yuans my heart skipped a beat because that was where Donny got ill. Now it's just me, you know, the end of the line and any kinda danger I just get scared...Christ. My life has been a wash-out pretty much, it doesn't mean yours has to go the same way. You see what I'm saying, right? If either of us should commit suicide, it should be me. I've been so scared of death that I've been afraid to live.'

'But that's the whole point of life,' said Robbie, 'that's why you have to seize every opportunity, every chance to make something of it. Otherwise it's just existence, just carrying on for the sake of it. Maybe that's why you're scared of death: because you don't feel you've achieved enough in your life to justify dying so soon.'

'No, I'm scared of death because I don't know what's on the other side. I'm scared of death because- because what if this is as good as it gets? What if I end up in Hell because of my failings in this world? What if there's nothing at all, just . . .' – she waved her hand vaguely –

91

'oblivion? Blackness? Existence has to be better than non-existence. Being alive has to be better than being dead.'

'Why?'

Alexa smiled. 'I guess I'm talking to the wrong person about how essential it is to be alive. I might as well talk to a cactus about how great it is in Lapland. Why is being alive so good? It's feeling, isn't it – it's the first breath of fresh air in the morning and the luxury of sleep in the night time. It's the sight of a sunset streaking the sky in the evening or the sight of a bird flying in the morning. It's laughing and crying. It's the feeling of a cool shower on a hot day, or a warm body next to yours on a cold night. It's hate and desperation and sadness. It's joy and success and love.' By this point, Alexa had moved round to Robbie's side of the table and taken his hand.

Robbie was awkward: was Alexa gearing towards declaring being in love with him, or was she just hinting at it in an attempt to win the discussion? He wasn't sure what to say in case it was the wrong answer. He sighed. This is why he'd wanted to become an actor: he wanted to do something creative, and he could enunciate and discuss well enough, but he didn't necessarily want to use his own words to do it with. He had his own thoughts, of course, what teenager doesn't? But to be able to articulate them: that was another matter entirely.

'I dunno Alexa. It's tough what you've been through: you must look at me and think at least I've got both parents, I haven't really had tragedy in my life at all. But it doesn't mean that I can't get depressed at being such a failure or anything. It doesn't mean I don't have any right to kill myself. Sure, joy and success and love and all that is wonderful, but it seems such a fucking effort to get it – I'm not sure that the pain and ardour and labour is worth the temporary gain that those things bring. I'm not convinced that I've had enough of it anyway in between the boredom and loneliness and frustration and the fucking tedium that life has brought me so far. It's hard to appreciate life when you're marooned in an 80-minute Geography lesson and the only thing to look forward to is going home and writing essays and listening to the radio and waiting for next morning and doing exactly the same thing again.'

Robbie paused, looking out at the sea through the windows of the bar. 'As for the future, I don't see anything to look forward to. You should stay alive if you still want to achieve what you want to. But I've come as far as I can. I think my acting's going to be underappreciated or just ignored – I don't want my only TV to be, y'know, a Tic-Tacs advert or some kids' sitcom. I don't want to be on stage just to be in the background in *West Side Story* and live destitute in London going 'Well, at least I'm in work!' Who would want that?'

'In that case, you're as scared of risk as I am,' drawled Alexa, behind a cloud of smoke. 'What a perfect couple we are. Anyway, where are we going again, and why?'

Chapter Seven

(I)

They were on one of the smaller islands off Papua New Guinea with the rest of the Club 1830 group, being led by Annie-Key Walker, who was explaining the outing.

'The New World was a strange one for explorers, in which they were meant to dispel the myths and legends surrounding the unchartered territories, but retain them too: made-up information of the "Here Be Monsters" variety which proved people's suspicions were given just as much weight as stuff like the potato, the pineapple and tobacco. That's why Barnum was so successful – he just made up things that he'd discovered on non-existent journeys, like the Fiji mermaid. Who was going to disprove him and go to Fiji to refute it?'

They continued through an area of rainforest as Annie-Key continued. Alexa unscrewed a hip-flask, batting away insect life as she did. 'Of course, as well as the sea-serpents and monsters, there was plenty to fear on land as well. Look at *The Lost World*: they had dinosaurs! Or the Yeti, of course, first reported in 1832. You still get it – the Chupacabras wasn't reported until 1995.'

They came onto a stretch of beach which looked onto the Bismarck Sea and onto the Pacific Ocean. Turning back, you could still make out the outline of the mainland, volcanic mountains rising above the cityscape. Alexa wondered what the point of all this was, whether Robbie had come here to be eaten by pterosauruses or tyrannoraptors or whatever they were called, it was Donny who had been into dinosaurs, not her.

'But the idea of giant women many feet tall was also a seductive one, women who supposedly lived in the Amazon thousands of years ago. There's no evidence for it, of course: no evidence that anyone who walked the Earth was particularly more gigantic than anyone who walks it now; in fact, if anything, the opposite's true, people are getting taller. That's why it's so hard to walk round an authentic Tudor pub without fracturing your skull.' Annie-Key was only 5'6,' still, the men amongst her saw her point.

'The only remaining proof is right here,' she added and suddenly the reason why they were there became obvious.

(II)

When Zan reached the afterlife, he was the only one on the soul train to have neither gone to Heaven nor Hell, which rendered him eligible for a position maintaining the fabric of reality in a dimension which was neither good nor bad, just eternal and necessary.

There were more possible roles available than one would think: Zan could have gone to work on the creation of new flora and fauna pending introduction to Earth. The casual onlooker would imagine that this position was in decline over the last 64 million years, with much of the world having been explored and most of the wildlife on

Earth having been discovered and/or hunted to extinction. In fact the employees were as busy as ever: those who worked there spent much of their time working on mutations and on ocean life, the majority of which had still gone undiscovered and looked even more unimaginably freaky than even the most surreal, vivid nightmare could suggest.

Alternatively, Zan could have been positioned with the Gods of Time, maintaining the rotation of Earth around the Sun, the maintenance of the passing of time across the universe. It would not have been suited to Zan, however, being as it was a largely administrative task based on mathematics and astrophysics. Only the intellectually enlightened were admitted, and that gate was closed to Zan.

Based on his life and his mentality, then, his soul was sent to the Angel of Death, who he had rarely met since. Death explained the nature and importance of the task that Zan would be given for eternity and how his collecting the souls of the universe was essential to the very running of the planet. The official name for the position was *psychopomp*, a name that Zan hated, finding it ridiculous and psychopompous. Some of the more austere death collectors still referred to themselves as psychopomps, but the industry slang, as it were, was banshee, which Zan far preferred. He liked Valkyrie too, but that was a specific term for those who collected fallen soldiers from the field of battle, a position that they'd been doing since the Greek times. He'd met the Valkyries – who were exclusively female – on numerous occasions and found that, despite the armoured breastplates and winged chariots that they still insisted on riding around in, they were perfectly level and decent characters.

As Astaroth had pointed out, collecting the dead was hardly a part-time job and Zan had been kept busy during his time in Limbo; a time before which he remembered almost nothing. Psychopomposis wasn't so bad; still, there were other areas of the afterlife which were beyond good and evil but which seemed equally, if not more, interesting. For example, if he had had a better knowledge of science beyond rudimentary pop-science, he could have worked in the Omniscience labs, which is where he was heading now.

Technically, the Omniscience laboratories fell under Gabriel's remit. In practise, they were mostly picked up by Ambrose, the patron saint of learning and, under his watch, worked as a sort of laboratory/library hybrid. All the information on anything, ever, was stored in its infinite capacity, but rather than being a sterile learning resource, it was alive with creation too: moulds and designs for new creations, both organic and technological; the conducting of experiments for new machinery.

The building's permanent residents were mostly scientists, architects and designers whose work had been seen as beneficial during their lifetime but had proven to be a total disaster when unleashed on Earth. The most famous resident, Zan had heard, was Thomas Midgeley, responsible for having added lead to petrol and for the compound chlorofluorocarbons, or CFCs, the ozone destroyer. Although Zan had never personally encountered him there, he had heard whispers that Dr Walter Freeman, the prolific, ice-pick wielding populariser of the lobotomy, was also condemned there, his work proving to have an uncertain position due to its success/failure/nothing happening ratio.

97

They were taken on following one of the Adherence To Policy meetings, during which Beelzebub had grumbled that he was 'weary of having to spit-roast by-the-book, pious, virtuous eggheads just because they invented something hideous that only turned out to be hideous 100 years later'. For example, while everybody agreed that CFCs were a bad thing, opinions differed on their creator: should a man be punished for his actions in his life when his intentions were good? It was universally agreed, for example, that ideas being manipulated or misused by scheming chancers couldn't be held as the responsibility of the person who had the initial idea – otherwise, the writers of the Bible would be off to Hell along with everyone else – but what about an invention which had actually been created and implemented? Eventually it was decided that they should go to the Omniscience laboratories and get on with testing and fine-tuning things that would be discovered and/or unleashed on the world in approximately the year 5000.

'Rare indeed it is that we see the plague wagons stopping here,' Ambrose greeted Zan, interrupting Zan's reverie.

'Nor is it in our habit to visit, the work of the psychopomp being without end and quite infinite, as I'm sure you can appreciate,' replied Zan, unconsciously dropping into the same linguistic patterns as Ambrose. He'd only met Ambrose once and briefly at that during his cursory show-round of the ethically neutral zones of the afterlife; still, he was at the centre of all possible knowledge for a reason. As a result, he decided against expressing any particular surprise that Ambrose had known he was arriving.

'Quite so; but it is good work that you are doing, Alessandro,' said Ambrose. 'Come in, do.'

'We are doing good work in a sort of ethically neutral way, definitely; I would rather consider it 'essential' than good I think,' said Zan. He was distracted, predictably, looking around at the chaos, the epic building a cavalcade of futuristic weapons and hideous monsters awaiting alignment to either the sea or a remote corner of outer space. He felt like a child in a toy shop created by the criminally insane: excited, fascinated but terrified. 'These weapons that you've created here – these just wait until someone's ready to invent them?'

'A succinct way of illustrating it, yes. We have a mass of creations here, as you can see: technology for thousands of years. However, while the inventions are ready for Earth, Earth is not yet ready for the inventions. The notion of the automobile in the Roman coliseums with which I was contemporaneous would be unthinkable, yet by the 1900s it was ready to be invented. On that note, have a look over here.'

Ambrose directed Zan's attention towards an aerodrome, in which various unidentifiable flying objects sat. Some flew above, tested out by aeronautic engineers and pilots. One of the vehicles currently in flight was–

'The flying car,' gasped Zan.

'Man is a curious species, Alessandro, of this I am sure you will agree. They have the ability to swim and to walk on land, yet they constantly strive for that which eludes them: the ability to fly. Consider the eagle: you don't see it wanting to swim, or building rafts to enable it to do so, yet the human wants to have it all. Now, by the 1800s, they had sufficiently developed their technology and their minds enough to justify introducing the aeroplane to the world. Before that, the aeroplane would have seemed baffling, unthinkable, a terrifying disaster. Now, as regards the flying car. Man has dreamt of the flying car since the 1900s, yet technology as late as the early 21st century was insufficient for it to become reality.'

'But it does become reality, right?' asked Zan.

'Earth receives the flying car at some point, yes,' confirmed Ambrose, 'but further explanation of how it works or indeed, when or how it appears on Earth, would likely be inconceivable to your late 20th Century, early 21st Century mind.'

'All I know is that I've never seen a flying car when I've been on Earth any time recently,' sighed Zan. 'Science fiction has lied to me.'

'Foolish is the man whose soothsayer is pulpy fantasy writing,' warned Ambrose.

'So how do you know that Earth isn't ready for technology like the flying car?'

'We had an unfortunate incident with the helicopter.'

'The helicopter?'

'You're familiar with the Nazca Lines in Peru?'

Zan nodded. The Nazca Lines were markings on the ground made hundreds of years before the birth of Christ, which could only be seen from above, despite the lack of contemporary aeronautic technology. They were constantly used as 'proof' of extraterrestrial visits to Earth, mostly by hippies who liked making up crackpot theories as far as Zan could tell.

'How about Ezekiel?' Ambrose added.

'Um. Well, Ezekiel was a prophet, wrote one of the last few books in the Old Testament. Book's kinda chatty, full of parables and prophecy if I remember right. God spends a lot of time talking in it. You'll have to help me out though, Doc. I was raised Catholic but it's been a long time since I read that particular chapter.'

'You remember how the book starts, though?'

'I don't even remember my graduation day, so I'm probably the wrong person to ask about anything that happened on Earth while I was still alive – but it's something pretty messed up, otherwise you wouldn't be asking me.'

'God appears to Ezekiel after Ezekiel has a vision of four creatures which flew around him and above Earth as a result of a 'dome made of dazzling crystal' and held some wheels. 'I heard the noise their wings made in flight; it sounded like the roar of the sea, like the noise of a huge army'.'

The idea rang a dim bell to Zan. 'And that was a helicopter?'

'We're omniscient, Alessandro, but we are not infallible unfortunately. Some klutz screwed up and put the helicopter in 600 BC rather than in 1900AD. Normally we only plant the genesis of an idea into an inventor's mind, but here, the helicopter was simply dropped off, in the same way as we sometimes introduce a new animal to the planet. Some Incas were able to get hold of the helicopter and managed to get it as far as Babylon before losing control and crashing it into the sea.'

'Isn't that thousands of miles? That's insane.'

'Thousands of miles, yes, insane, no. The *idea* of a helicopter is more powerful than an actual helicopter, which is hindered by the physical limitations of Earth in terms of its weight, speed, resistance and velocity. A conceptual helicopter could – did! –travel that far, at a speed which must have been terrifying. Of course, we were able to organise a recovery mission for the helicopter and repress the evidence, but the idea has always lived on. That's why it features in Ezekiel and why the Chinese were talking about some of the rudimentaries as far back as 400BC.'

'I thought the things that turned up in Ezekiel were totally different, weren't they four-headed wheels or some such?'

'You have to account for mistranslation and metaphorical subtlety, to say nothing of the fact that if you saw something flying anachronistically overhead 2,000 years before it was supposed to, your memory might be a little hazy when it came to writing it down. Ezekiel did his best to try and explain what he'd just seen, but how could he? This is why the helicopter wasn't invented in 600BC, you see: not only was the concept completely alien to the people of that time, when it arrived, they didn't even understand what its component parts were! This is why we can't simply put things on Earth willy-nilly: Earth needs to be ready for them first, through practice, through trial and error, through sophistication of both theory and practice.'

'And the Nazca Lines?'

'Depressed at the disappearance of two of their own, the Incas built the Nazca Lines as a sort of 'X marks the spot' so that, if the pilots returned from their intrepid mission, they would know where they were going.'

'Oh'. Zan was getting nowhere in his mission. He suspected Ambrose knew why he'd come, being that this was the epicentre of omniscience and all, so why were they wasting time chatting about helicopters and flying cars and Biblical prophets? The answer came to him as soon as he thought it: Because Ambrose wants someone to talk to, that's why. It must be lonely in a way, when the only people you talk to know everything. But then, maybe there you're assuming that a saint has desires, or envy.

Come on, Zan, get on with your job. But all right, one more question. Not just because curiosity is killing being in this joint, but because of a professional integrity to show a genuine interest in the work of the people who you're visiting.

'All this work seems pretty noble, Ambrose. But this has to be the same place where Agent Orange and napalm and the atom bomb were created. So why give them to humans?'

'Well, don't forget that God gave man free will, so if he wishes to use these inventions, he will and we can't intervene,' replied Ambrose. 'We can't concern ourselves with ethics here, remember: we're neutral.'

'But you're a saint!'

'Yes, but the demon Phenex is of equal footing to me here. One cannot take sides in the pursuit of knowledge. If man has an idea to use some dreadful machine or weapon, the idea will linger on until it is finally constructed and destroyed. Better for man to find out for himself the ghastly effects of napalm or of the nuclear missile than for divine intervention. Still, that's us; what can we do for you?'

'I'm looking for information about someone.'

'I see. Well, that's no problem, we'll simply fire up the Metatron and have a look what we can find.'

The Metatron was a fiendishly complicated and devilishly intricate machine, monolithic in stature. Despite the numerous unfeasibly advanced and sophisticated devices and gadgets that the Omniscience labs were full of, the Metatron looked for all the world like the control panel of a 1960s space station.

'Technically this information is based on abstract concepts floating in the ether and we could choose any physical representation of it that we like,' Ambrose was saying. 'This appeared to be the best way of doing it. I mean, yes, it looks slightly ridiculous but it still has a quaint antique charm while being functional enough to actually work – now who was it you were looking for?'

'Guy called Robbie Adams, I think he is – or was, or will be, whatever – from Hartlepool.' Zan gave an approximate birth year based on his age at the time of the prayer Gabriel had given him.

'Hmmm,' mused Ambrose. 'We've got a tenuous link here to someone called Alexa Ribiera, you can see her birth year here, date of death – unknown? I really should get the Metatron through maintenance, it's all very well for mortals to see through a glass darkly but it doesn't quite cut it here, does it?'

'Um, no, I guess not, but it's not Alexa I'm here to find out about,' segued Zan smoothly. 'What about this Robbie, what's his date of death?'

'Is this one of your missions, Zan? If it is, surely the details would have already been made available to you?'

'I'm doing my homework early, let's have a look at the card.' Zan read the details of the date and place of death. And if that was where Robbie was, and if he was associated with Ribiera, and Ribiera was immortal, there was a pretty good chance of catching her there.

Zan moved on. 'Thanks Doc, I got a soul train to catch.'

They were staring at an enormous pair of breasts.

Alexa shook her head. How utterly typical of one of Robbie's schemes. Never trust the imagination of a teenage boy with money, that's all there was to be said about it.

The breasts, then, were not just some over-inflated silicone nasties sported by a topless model or pornographic actress but a pair which must have stood eight foot tall themselves, like Stonehenge imagined by Russ Meyer. They were dislodged from any chest, standing as they were lodged against one another and standing weirdly firm and pert despite their apparently ancient age.

'These are the only existing evidence of giants having walked the earth,' said Annie-Key. 'Of course, they appear in mythology all the time: the Cyclops, the Nefilim, Jack and the Beanstalk, but there's never been any evidence that these aren't just projected fears. Except, of course, for these, which have baffled anthropologists, cryptozoologists and historians alike.'

'Cryptozoologists?' asked Alexa, but Robbie made hushing gestures.

'Portuguese and Spanish explorers visiting the islands in the 1500s were told that this was the remainder of a great battle between the last surviving giant women. It must have played like one of those fights in a Godzilla movie. During a lengthy battle between the two of them, one cut the other's breasts off with a single stroke. At least, that's what we think they were told: the explorers mention the breasts in diaries but never officially reported it to Spain and they largely remained semi-mythical for years, until the island's colonisation late in the Victorian era. At that point, the colonials found it and it became a phenomenon amongst the rich and eccentric for a time. A tourists' delight, as it were.'

'So this has been verified, then? It really is a pair of giant boobs?' said someone.

'All the records on it suggest that it is. There's not a great deal of paperwork concerning it though, even the Internet's quiet about it: it's a low-key phenomenon hardly anybody believes and, as a result, scientific research on it has been limited. Apparently, there's a Mask of Tutankhamen-style curse myth surrounding it, which has scared a lot of people away.'

'See, that always sounded like bullshit to me,' muttered Alexa. 'A bunch of guys from the 1900s are now all dead? Doesn't sound too much of a curse to me, you know?'

'I did consider climbing into a sarcophagus in a pyramid when I compiled the Ten Places To Die,' whispered Robbie. 'But then I realised there weren't any left in pyramids and they were all on display in British museums.'

Annie-Key was still talking. 'You've also got the problem of a lot of natives worshipping it as a fertility symbol, so they're leery about it being researched in too great a depth. Worried that scientific evaluation will destroy the power it holds? Or worried that it'll be exposed as a sham? Whatever, here it is: one of the great hidden treats of the Victorian era.'

The group gathered around the boobs, which were protected by a sheer cliff-face on one side and a steel barricade around the rest. Astonishingly well-preserved considering their unfathomable age, but other than that, well, it was a pair of breasts, simple as that. The contours, the shape, the colouring, the proportions: it couldn't be anything else.

'So what's your brilliant plan here, Robbie?'

'I dunno, I thought look around the beach a bit, then get some lunch. I don't think dinner for our group is scheduled until about 7pm-'

'No, I mean, why are we here? We've not come for the company or the sight-seeing, after all.'

'Well, we'll stay here overnight. We'll come back when there's nobody around and jump the barrier, then I'll go and be smothered by the boobs.'

'Why can't you just jump off the cliff?' asks Alexa, pointing.

'Then it's just another cliff-based death plunge. I could aim to land on the boobs, but knowing my luck I'd hit my head on the barricade instead. Anyway, I think there's some sort of private land up there, which-'

'-Is going to be harder to break into than an ancient fertility symbol which is fiercely protected?' finished Alexa. 'You know, if you wanted to die by breast-based suffocation, you could have just used my tits.'

'Hey, we've been through this. You didn't want your life extended so that you could spend it in prison,' retorted Robbie.

A pause. 'This is it, you know,' said Alexa. 'This is the last of the Ten Places To Die. None of them have achieved what you wanted to achieve, have they? What are you gonna do if this backfires?'

Robbie thought. She was right – it hadn't worked as well as he'd hoped. 'We can go home, I guess. I haven't heard of anything else that would replace it. Go back to

Cemetery Drive and plot our next move, I suppose. But it's not going to happen, is it? You're right, this is it. Anyway, come on: I don't suppose there's any chance I can, y'know, get laid one last time before I die?'

'Last of the romantics, I see,' drawled Alexa. 'Anyway' she said, turning to follow him, 'you said that the last nine times.'

Chapter Eight

(I)

I was up horribly early – it must have been ten in the morning – and listening to a death jam played on local radio which appeared to be by discredited crooner Millie Kennedy. I had long forgotten the controversy about Kennedy, having little interest in popular culture; the only reason I was listening to local radio at all was as an experiment into whether there could be a proven link between short-distance radio waves and the destruction of brain cells. This was working on the hypothesis that the radio station itself, where the radio waves were inevitably more concentrated, appeared to hire without exception the most mindless drones ever to have been employed in a public speaking capacity. Surely our education system has not failed us to the extent that trite chatter like this passes as the zenith of broadcasting in the area, I thought. Therefore, it stood to reason that the imbecility was caused by some sort of radio frequency, leaving people only able to create prank calls and Guess The Year slots as a way of filling the time on their shows. That was the hypothesis anyway. To carry out the experiment, I had secreted rodents across the city at various intervals in the station's wavelength, including a few in the station itself thanks to a telecommunications engineer who owed me a favour. I was hoping that, should the experiment fail, the mice might at least be discovered and the station closed down for health and safety reasons.

Needless to say this was not the only thing occupying my mind this morning: much more local radio and I feared I'd become the listener who phoned in and shouted 'It's 1996, now stop wasting my time, you insolent bunch of cretins.' I was also working on general maintenance to the magic carpet and attempting to organise an entirely clean Internet setting for the Technonomicon, dreading to think what was going to happen to the damn thing if it caught a virus. No doubt it was going to be something minor like the destruction of the entire planet, but I couldn't afford to take the risk. I was also trying to work the Google Camirror, a webcam built into the Technonomicon. I wasn't too bothered about the fact that it existed at all – indeed, it had its advantages, of this there was no doubt. The problem was more its attitude towards actually working: the damn thing kept turning itself on, recording the footage that it was screening without my knowledge, then saving it in memory-clogging files which saved in some obscure location then refused to delete. As yet, I'd been confident that it hadn't then uploaded itself to some remote server for publication across the Internet, but I wasn't prepared to take the risk.

Normally I'd lumber Francisco with tedious tasks like this but, as I've mentioned before, the asinine acolyte had gotten himself pregnant and as an employer, I was legally obliged to give him maternity leave. I had, of course, offered to arrange alternative solutions to retain his service and rid us of any baby squalling, but he'd turned into a proper hen about it.

I warmed up the soldering iron in the hope of applying solder to the parts of the magic carpet which needed it and was just about to apply the first blob of solder when time stopped.

I sighed. 'If you're going to march in here without explanation or introduction, Zan, can you at least *not* do it while I'm in this position and obviously busy.'

The psychopomp had managed to lumber a Valkyrie, Brunhilde, with whatever tasks he usually did. It seems that there'd been a ceasefire in the African civil war which she'd been working on and, whilst the ceasefire was expected to last for less than 72 hours, Zan had given his word that when fighting broke out again, he'd stop off and collect all the civilians whose homes had been burnt to the ground or who had been shot accidentally in military 'friendly fire'. It didn't seem like my kettle of fish, but in the world Zan lived in, it was at least something different from the drudgery of an eternity with the robe and scythe dragging middle-aged old bats to the afterlife. Zan had arrived here in a bad way, having traipsed around for ages without successfully capturing Alexa Ribiera. All this, though, I found out later; his first words to me were:

'Robbie Adams.'

'Oh, what, who?' I sighed. 'Was he the jerk who did that song from the Robin Hood movie?'

'No, there's some sort of association with Alexa Ribiera. Who is he? Where is he now?'

Meanwhile, at the same time –

'I'm such a loser that I even fail at committing suicide,' moped Robbie.

Oh, he'd got over the barrier alright. He'd gotten to the monoliths (duoliths?) without any problem, presumably because nobody assumed that he'd have had the sheer bloody cheek to have simply strolled over to the ancient national wonders, which is, of course, exactly what he had done. He had touched them and been impressed by their firmness, their tenderness. Sure, they were pretty cold, but it was night and they were thousands of years old and dead, why wouldn't they have been?

But as he lay down, lifted up one of the colossal breasts and dropped it onto himself, as he started to choke for air, as he started to choke on sawdust, he . . . hang on, sawdust? He realised it was coming out of the breast itself, that behind the outer layer of breast tissue was nothing more than padding and falsehood. Even the tissue itself, he supposed, could have been made out of whale blubber or something equally huge, and preserved in the same way as an actual breast would be. The monument was a sham; dying here would cruelly expose that – or maybe not, maybe he'd be found by the next person responsible for padding this thing and thrown into the sea, after which he'd be forgotten. Maybe there'd be a mystery when his body washed ashore months later with no identity and an international hunt for identification would start up, and . . . no, no this was ridiculous, nothing he wanted to achieve here would work. He climbed out of the bosom of the, er, bosom, threw his suicide note into the sea and walked back to Alexa, shaking his head. At this point he finally detonated the obviously worn-out motion-detector spotlights and alerting guards, leaving them to sprint into the rainforest and thrash through the paths, clattering into brambles and allowing sleepy mosquitoes to feed on their wounds, carrying each other when they stumbled over fiendish branches and back into the hotel.

112

Now they were back in Club 1830's company on the ferry taking the long journey back to Britain, a journey they were lucky still had tickets available, having not booked a return trip.

Annie-Key saw Alexa and Robbie moping and came over. 'Hi, you two, how did you enjoy the New Guinea Cleavage? It's not something you see every day, is it?'

Robbie looked up. 'Yeah, it's definitely unique. What are your feelings on it, Annie-Key? You reckon it's legit?'

'It's not really my place to comment on whether something is or isn't real; I just show you guys what's there and let you fill in the blanks,' smiled Annie-Key, taking a seat next to them. 'For what it's worth, though, off the record, I think that it's unlikely. The ferocity with which people protect those things from a proper, rigorous scientific examination is ridiculous if they're real. It's pretty cool anyway, in the same way that a magic trick isn't any less amazing once you know how it's done. But anyway, who am I to comment? I'm off to Fiji to scope out a location. Apparently there's been rumours of genuine mermaids off the coast, and failing that, there might be a manatee colony around there and that would be a sight to see. You know they were mistaken for mermaids?'

'Yeah, I do know. We're chasing Death,' Robbie confessed.

Annie-Key eyed Robbie with a mild interest, instead of the baffled horror that he was expecting. 'Death, eh? You know, I did cryptozoology for about a year, employed by some university in Indiana. I spent my time looking at mythical creatures and their basis in reality.'

'Oh, so THAT's what cryptozoology is,' interrupted Alexa. 'You look at made-up stuff like unicorns.'

'Yeah, unicorns, chupacabras, Yeti, Loch Ness Monsters, all that stuff. But I never even bothered with studying the personification of Death. I mean, surely that's not what you mean? It's not literal Death you're looking for?'

Robbie and Alexa explained their story.

'Hmm. Okay. Can I ask you something?' asked Annie-Key, having heard the tale up unto this point.

'Sure.'

'How do you even know Death's actually pursuing you? It's not as if you're in some sort of *Final Destination* adventure. You're aggressively pursuing Death, not the other way round. For that matter, how do you know Death even exists? How do you know that there's even an afterlife?'

'I'm sorry?' asked Alexa. 'A woman who goes round chasing Bigfoot is asking me to be sceptical?'

Annie-Key smiled and held her hands out. 'I'm just trying to understand. All these mythological creatures I've looked at, all the history I've explored and the bears I've run after thinking I'd finally found the Yeti, they had some sort of basis in reality, there was tangible evidence for at least *something* physical causing the confusion. I mean, what you believe is up to you, of course. But it sounds to me as if you'd have as much luck chasing the pot of gold at the end of the rainbow.'

Robbie said nothing. In truth, he had been thinking along much the same lines for a few of the last couple of the Ten Places To Die: for the first time in a life he had generally considered worthless he had found himself pretty much content, exploring the world with a hot woman in tow. When, for example, he'd applied to the Magic Circle with the intention of having Alexa doing the

114

clichéd 'saw you in half' trick, and incinerating himself while still in the box. The trick, which was, in typical Adams fashion, under-rehearsed and poorly thought out, had inevitably failed, leading to an equally inevitable lecture from Alexa as they returned to their motel on the outskirts of Las Vegas. But was there a part of him that was glad? Surely not, no; but then, what guarantee was there that Death would be waiting for them on the other side? What sort of afterlife would be preferable to this anyway? If death was just the end and Alexa had dodged it, then she was immortal and the idea of some sort of spiritual being was stupid.

But then, Robbie and Alexa had both been raised to believe in Heaven and Hell, so . . .

'So you wanna know why I think Death is coming for me?' asked Alexa. 'It's in my dreams, it's the first thing I see when I close my eyes at night and the last thing I see before I wake up.'

'What is?'

'Oblivion. Empty nothingness, that's all my dreams are. Just blackness, dead air. I used to dream every night before the bank raid. I remembered every dream as well, vividly. It was like my dreams were compensating for the fact that I wasn't doing fuck-all in my life. Now there's just a void.'

'You don't think that this is because you've actually been living?'

'It's not that. The night my mother died, I had dreams. The night I bought my own home, I had dreams. The night I lost my virginity, I had dreams. The night I had a near-death experience, I didn't. I don't think that's coincidence, I think that's my being told I shouldn't be here.'

'And the photo thing,' added Robbie.

'Yeah, and the photo thing.'

(II)

After dinner Annie-Key approached Alexa and Robbie.

'So I was thinking this afternoon about what you guys were planning to do – meet Death and all that. It put me in mind of things like prayer and black magic. Depending on what you want to invoke, of course. So I did a bit of research on it and I think I might be able to help.'

'I realised I could ride the ship's Internet connection from my laptop and from there, check out some of the forums and sites that I'd looked at back when I was looking at the dark arts,' she explained shortly afterwards in her cabin, Robbie and Alexa sat besides her on the bed. 'I hadn't looked at these sites for years. Some of them were dead, some redirected to spam sites and some were taken over with loony conspiracy theories about black magic in the Googleplex, but I did find a few things of interest. I think I've found a ritual, a ceremony, whatever, which you could use.'

'That's great, Annie-Key. Can you help us?'

'Well, I'm more into research, investigation, scientific methodology than I am demonology and cabbalistic witchcraft,' replied Annie-Key. 'On the other hand, I wasn't up to much this evening, so why not?'

(III)

Back in Britain Zan was pacing around, and was just about to take a seat on the monstrous chaise-lounge I'd acquired from a clearout sale of Aleister Crowley's house.

'Don't sit on that one, it'll eat you alive,' I warned.

'I'm a metaphysical being, I'm already dead,' drawled Zan.

'It doesn't know that and couldn't care less anyway.' It being magical, the chaise-lounge ate whatever it felt like and could exist on the same plane as Zan, as human beings, and as the invisible creatures who lurk in the corners of rooms that only cats can see. 'If you don't want to be reduced to metaphysical cinders I'd sit somewhere else.'

He slumped in an armchair. 'Anyway, listen up. I'm not just trying to dodge the bullet from the Angel of Death now, I'm starting to get Time on my ass. You know why? I'll tell you. You're familiar with the idea that Nature abhors a vacuum and that the very continuation of space-time itself is based on everything in its right place? You know that if something is in the wrong place, the wrong situation, then something else must fill that role? Well, can you imagine what happens if something doesn't die, but is supposed to? From that point forth the space that that thing or person is occupying should have been occupied by something or someone else. I'm sure I shouldn't have to tell you, but that means right now that Alexa Ribiera is living somebody else's life. At the same time as she avoided death, the person who was set to do

117

whatever it is that she is doing dropped dead, for no understandable reason.'

'How do you even know that, though?' I asked.

'Because the woman's only in Christing Limbo, isn't she?' Zan shouted. 'She didn't meet the criteria to be a banshee like me, so she went over to the Timelords for an interview! Those freaking know-it-alls knew something was up, since they didn't have anyone scheduled in to interview and you can imagine what their diaries look like. So they did some fishing around and sure enough the woman's died when she's not supposed to have done.'

(IV)

Down a previously unthinkable staircase went Annie-Key, Alexa and Robbie. Down, down into the dark heart of the ship, through an increasingly labyrinthine corridor system where no human seemed to ever have passed by. Down here the lights hummed and flickered intermittently, only adding to the tension of the deserted electric-Marie-Celeste feel of the whole set-up. Another left and Annie-Key stopped at an unmarked door. She gave the nod to Alexa and Robbie, turned a key in a lock and they were pushing the door open to reveal . . .

'Why would you have a conference room on a ship?'

'It's a luxury cruise ship, it's perfectly possible that there's going to be some corporate get-togethers happening once in a while, I guess,' said Annie-Key, walking into the facilities, decorated with beige wallpaper, forgettable landscape prints and baize tablecloths. Beneath their feet, an ochre carpet with jaunty naval anchors slumped across the floor. Against the wall, bottles of mineral water and cordial stood atop a cabinet.

'Anyway, be grateful: to conduct this particular spell we needed a room which was completely lifeless and I think we've got one.'

Robbie nodded. 'So what's the plan?'

'Well, it's technical. When you're aiming to summon an angel or a saint, or entice the Virgin Mary to listen to your prayers, you need a very holy collection: holy water, crosses, that sort of thing. When you're trying to entice Satan to your black magick shindig you tend to prefer things like pentagrams and bloody sacrifices. The one thing both ceremonies seem to have in common is candles. So, using this logic, if you want to invoke Death you have to surround yourself with the dead or deathly. Now, I've been limited in what I could get for this by what happened to be in the shop's ships . . . sorry, the ship's shops, but I've done the best I can here.'

Annie-Key pulled out the artefacts that she'd prepared for the invocation:

- A Troy Fettle paperback, *The Spatchcock of Poussin*. Fettle you may remember from his previous gung-ho spy books set in the Cold War, such as *The Russian Resolution*, but the common opinion was that he'd been phoning it in for some time now with a series of increasingly second-rate novels, belying the fact that he was more preoccupied with his computer game series *Jack Steel In The Hour Of Chaos*. This particular book, about a spy who receives a mysterious message

119

concealed in a French restaurant's main course before embarking on a gung-ho killing spree disguised as a race against time to save the planet, was described variously as 'soulless' and 'arriving DOA': descriptions strangely absent from the book cover.

-   The latest DVD from film mogul Samuel Goldman, *Sarah's Gotta Split*, a ghastly pun on the film's setting, Split in Croatia.

('I thought this was meant to be his best work for years?' Robbie asked.

'Don't believe the hype, kid,' Alexa grimaced, having seen it while it was on rental.

Annie-Key nodded in agreement. 'Yeah, this is a lifeless movie alright'.)

-   A microwaveable chicken fillet. Nobody had any arguments there.
-   A bunch of candles. As Annie-Key pointed out, candles were consistent in both sanctified and diabolic ceremony, so it couldn't harm any to use them.
-   A box of chalk.

'So what are we supposed to be doing with all this stuff, Annie?' asked Robbie, while stood on a chair disconnecting the smoke alarm in the room.

Annie-Key took one of the tablecloths off the table and lay it on the floor. Taking a piece of chalk from the box, she knelt down and started to draw.

'Well, as I've said, Death lies somewhere between Heaven and Hell on the good-evil scale, right? I know you guys might not agree but death is a part of life neither good nor bad, the same as birth. So –who do we want to summon Death for here? – All right, Robbie, come over here. So, if you lie down on this tablecloth like so, it's about six foot seven Robbie, so we should have a bit of room for manoeuvre – I'll draw a cross here, Alexa, if you can draw a pentagram at the bottom there?'

'Yeah, sure. Hey, I brought some red wine, by the way.'

'That's good! Red wine is used in the Christian communions and by Satanists, so that's a good call.'

'It is?' Alexa and Robbie exchanged a glance. Robbie grinned. Alexa grinned back.

'Robbie,' continued Annie-Key, 'if you could take the deathly artefacts, Alexa and I will get the candles lit.'

Annie-Key and Alexa set up the candles to surround Robbie and started to light them. Alexa lit a cigarette while she was at it. Robbie lay, arms folded against his chest, holding the trashy pop culture artefacts and the microwave meal.

'This is going in the postcard. Or the essay 'What I Did In My Holidays',' said Robbie. 'This summer I attempted to summon spiritual beings in a boat's conference room while holding a chicken fillet.'

Robbie and Alexa giggled.

'Look, if you're gonna take the piss I'll leave you to find your own spiritual beings,' said Annie-Key, but she was smiling too. 'That said, I can't stay here too much longer anyway. Given how most satanic rituals supposedly turn out, summoning Death can have dire consequences for the people in the room and, since I'm neither dead nor wishing to be dead, I think I'll duck out at this point. I've got the spell that you need written here.'

Annie-Key handed Alexa a sheet of paper with the spell written down. It was in capital letters, but Annie-Key's writing was dreadful.

121

'Can you – I dunno, can you spell some of these words out for me?'

'OK – this one is 'angelus', this is 'nex'– I've gotta be careful of saying too many of these words at once in case I get sucked into the afterlife or something. You know, we might not have the opportunity to speak again. It's been interesting having you with us at Club 1830 – if you survive, we'll see you in Fiji, maybe?'

'If we survive, we'll see you for breakfast,' said Alexa. 'Robbie's got a chicken fillet he'll cook up.'

'OK, you guys take care. I'll get the light on the way out.' With that, Annie-Key was gone, leaving Alexa and Robbie alone by candlelight.

Alexa grinned. 'You know, this is insane. Most couples have a room, a bottle of wine, a DVD, candles, they're about to be romantic. You and I have the same thing and we're about to raise hell.'

'Hey, nobody ever said ours was a conventional relationship. Are you scared?'

'I don't know. Look, what if this doesn't work? What if nothing happens?'

'Well, nobody ever said it was guaranteed to work. I'd be willing to believe that we're marked men in existential terms, though, so it'll wake SOMETHING up. And if we don't invoke the Kraken, Chthulu, Leviathan or Poseidon I'd say we're one step closer to your immortality, right?'

'OK. Let's try it.' Alexa took a drink of the red wine she'd brought and began reading. 'Voco . . . angelus . . .'

Behind them the bottles of cordial and water began to shake as Alexa continued reciting the spell.

'. . . corruptio . . . everto?' hazarded Alexa.

Smoke rose from the ground and light shot up around Robbie. Colours spiralled above him at a dazzling speed, eventually resolving themselves into the shape of a figure.

In the same instance in a different time zone, across the world, Zan pricked up his ears at the sound of knocking.

'You hear something?' he asked.

'No,' I replied.

The figure that stepped out of the portal which floated above Alexa and Robbie had flowing locks and a ruffled shirt but appeared to be shrouded in darkness.

'WHO DARES SUMMON ME FROM THE GREAT BEYOND?!' it boomed, a guttural rumble whose bassy frequencies made the floor vibrate beneath them. 'FOR YEARS I HAVE SLEPT WITH NO DISTURBANCE. WHO HAS THE NERVE TO AWAKEN ME? Hey, this sound effect is pretty cool, isn't it? You can imagine it over a soul rhythm. Check it out. BABY I JUST GOTTA GET DOWN WITH YA . . . Ah, I can tell this material is wasted on this audience.'

Not having expected the spell to work, Alexa was frozen in a combination of terror, horror and, increasingly, bewilderment.

Robbie spoke first. 'Are . . . are you Death?'

'Uh, no?' said the figure, rolling a ball of flame across his fingers. 'Man, I know I didn't have much time to prepare for this summoning but I didn't realise I was looking THAT bad.' The flame returned to his palm and increased in size.

'I didn't say you were looking bad,' said Robbie quickly. 'Er, quite the opposite actually – of all the monstrous entities I've ever summoned you're definitely the best-looking. But, with no disrespect to you, we were trying to summon Death.'

'You got the spell wrong, then, didn't you? What you should have done is check the incantation before you said it.I OUGHT TO SEND YOU INTO THE FIERY DEPTHS OF HELL FOR DARING TO TRY IT!'

'Hey, in my defence,' Alexa managed, 'I was reading a non-native language in an indecipherable handwriting.'

'Give me that,' said the demon, stepping down from his floating position and walking over to Alexa, seizing the spell. 'Hm, I see what you mean – looking at this, I would have summoned myself too. Anyway, this spell's bollocks whoever would have said it. This pidgin Latin shit, man. You might as well say Abracadabra.' He took the bottle of red wine away from Alexa. 'You know, you really shouldn't drink this, it's bad for your heart. Or maybe it's good for your heart in moderation, I can't remember.'

'So who are you, then?' asked Robbie.

'I'm Astaroth. One of the SEVEN PRINCES OF HELL, prince of accusators and inquisitors, four staff under me-pretty sweet deal all things told. I tell you, I'm not surprised that I never get summoned anymore if the spell that successfully summons me is some mumbo-jumbo attached to the Grim Reaper. I've gotta sort that out with whoever wrote that book of spells and invocations – I mean, who's gonna be actively searching Death?'

'Ash, what are you doing over here?' remarked a voice behind the portal.

124

'I'm kinda in the middle of something here, Beelzebub,' Astaroth replied, turning to face the portal again.

'You're doing a summoning, aren't you? Let me see.'

'Oh fuck you, man, you're not my father.'

'Yeah, and hail Satan for that, but let's see. I don't want you making it look like Hell has gone soft.' At that point Beelzebub came through the portal. 'What's going on here?' he asked *sotto voce*. 'You've been here minutes and nothing's on fire?'

'Yeah, well check the surroundings Bub. When I first got here I actually sort of thought I was still in Hell already.'

'WHO DARES SUMMON THE DEMONS OF HELL?!' roared Beelzebub, head a dreadful skull, sending jets of fire rocketing to the ends of the room.

'Um, we did. But we didn't mean to, if that makes it any better,' asked Robbie. 'Um- would you like this chicken as a sacrifice, Oh Infernal One? Or, um, this book?'

'I OUGHT TO ROAST YOU OVER A FIRE FOR YOUR INSOLENCE, YOU IMPUDENT WRETCH!' screamed Beelzebub. Robbie and Alexa were clinging to each other in terror now. 'See, this is how you do a summoning, none of this wussy shit that you were pulling,' he said to Astaroth, cuffing him around the head.

'The summoning was going peachy until you interrupted,' retorted Astaroth, indignant. 'Anyway, these guys are after Death: it's no surprise their sacrifices are second-rate.'

'Death?' frowned Beelzebub. 'These wouldn't be the fellows Zan's after, would it?'

'Well, I hadn't asked, but yeah, probably.'

'Hm. Shame he's away pissing about on Earth with that technomage otherwise I'd bring him over.'

'I thought he said it was kind of important though? In fact, didn't we say that?'

'Yeah. But on the other hand, we're demons, and chaos is funny.'

'Listen, while you're here, do you know how we can summon Death?' asked Robbie.

Back at the house, I really wanted Zan to go home or at least somewhere which wasn't in my general vicinity. All this proximity to death was making my head hurt. 'So what do you think you can do to capture this woman, for once and for all?' I asked.

'I was hoping you'd tell me that,' he responded.

'Well, there's only one opportunity that you've got of getting your hands on Alexa.'

'All right,' sighed Astaroth. 'Listen, if you believe that the best way of getting Death or whoever off your back is to confront them directly, then you'll gain nothing by trying to summon the Grim Reaper using second-rate downloaded magick spells in a place thousands of miles away from home. Really there's only one way of doing it – one time and place you'd be able to do it.'

'And that is?'

'Go back to the time that it was meant to happen and meet them there.'

'How?'

'How?' I asked. 'Well, you're Death aren't you? Or at least, his representative. The laws of time and space don't apply to you, which is why we're sitting in frozen time here whilst you're telling me all this. If you were told to go and collect the corpses from the Battle of Hastings you'd have no difficulty doing it. So why don't you just nip back there and sort it out?'

'How? I've already been there. It didn't work. I can't go there again because the rules state that I can only be in the same place and the same time once. I've already blown that idea,' said Zan.

'Yeah, but say you arrived into that bank at 11.13. Why don't you just turn up at 11.12, do this whole time-stopping parlour trick you're so fond of and grab them then?'

'How?' Astaroth asked.

'Don't forget they're not governed by the same laws we are, Ash – they can't just travel through time and space whenever they feel like it!' hissed Beelzebub.

'Well, we could help them out. Grant a wish. Introduce them to Zan, something like that . . .'

'Yeah, but we're demons, we're not going to, are we? As for Zan, screw him. Let him make his own mistakes.'

'Oh yeah. Shit. I dunno, I was joking. Weren't you?'

Beelzebub sighed. 'This is the last summoning you do, Ash.'

Chapter Nine

Monday and Tuesday passed in a deadening binge of engineering and cybersex. I spent Wednesday battling with new Pro-Orchestra technology that had been requested by the Musician's Union.

I was working on the new sport of Warchestra, which is old hat nowadays but was, at the time, a radical new development to get the young and lower classes into classical music which had been a blazing success. Warchestra took the classical performance out of the stuffy halls that it was performed in to rapt silence in the 1900s and into 20,000 seater stadiums across the world. Two orchestras would each play for 45 minutes in an attempt to become winners of the Classical League. During these forty-five minutes, the performers had the opportunity to pick from a loaded substitutes bench. For example, if a rendition of Gymnopedie No 1 had gone down like a lead balloon, the conductor, impassive from the dug-out, could bring on a choir and smash out a crowd-pleasing 'Ode To Joy' in order to nudge them ahead. Classical purists bemoaned the fact that the music of kings had become obsessed with money and showboating and certainly the £130m transfer of violin maestro Luigi Lasagnizzi from the NY Symphony to the moneybags Madrid would underline that (all for nothing, alas: Lasagnizzi spent much of the season out with RSI). But its result was to take a genre of music which teenagers across the world had been desperately bored by at school and take its backbiting, its internal politics and its petty jealousies public. What schoolboy now could not listen to Rachmaninoff's Hungarian Rhapsody and successfully identify it as the passage with which the London Symphony Orchestra had won the World Cup with – in the last minute of extra time and in the Munich Superbowl, no less?

Anyway, I digress, you know all this anyway. The point of my work was to monitor every single member of the orchestra on the amount of time spent playing, the force of their strokes and the fluidity of their movement. These would then calculated on a spreadsheet and monitored in order to gauge the most essential and least essential members of the orchestra in preparation for their stadium concerts across the world. The plan was to attach to each orchestra member's shirts a small imp trapped in a computer chip, which would feedback the information required to a large computer system straight out of an Arthur C Clarke novel, which would then print off the data. Doubtless this would be derided in the public by cynical conductors such as Willie Connelly, Stockport United Orchestra's dour long-term sticksman, or playboy fly-by-night Gianfranco Hernandez. These same conductors, however, would do so while they were privately phoning each other demanding to know how they could acquire the talents of each other's industrious bassoonist or cor anglais virtuoso.

Come on, you didn't expect some geeks would actually sit there monitoring every single player for how many touches they made, did you? What a joke.

The point of all this is to make sure you're absolutely clear on how my time was being eaten up with perfecting this technology, how I would have temporarily forgotten

Zan's show-stopping (or at least, time-stopping) appearances and why I was so surprised when, on Thursday, Robbie and Alexa turned up at my door. I had, of course, met Alexa several times and entertained her at my house to demonstrate the flawlessness of my work and the justification for my competitively-priced salary, which is no doubt why she chose to bother me there. Robbie, on the other hand, was new to me and I naturally presumed that there'd been some sort of undisclosed son Alexa had hitherto kept schtum, or that the surly-looking youth had been asked to do community service by traipsing around keeping her amused. The two of them were both looking exhausted, as if they'd just finished a long journey and hadn't yet gone home and stuck the kettle on.

'Come in, come in,' I greeted, leaving Warchestra replays blaring to themselves on the permanently malfunctioning Sky+ box thing I had. 'Goodness knows I've not got anything else to worry about other than your adventures.'

'Hang on, I've not passed this way in months,' objected Alexa, stepping into the hallway, 'and the amount of money I put your way, I should be expecting your service for life.'

'I think he means,' managed the boy, whom I'd already assumed incapable of speech, being a teenager and all, 'that he's had more than one visitor calling about it. I'm Robbie, by the way.'

'Robbie? And you are, of course, Alexa's . . .'

'Boyfriend,' finished Robbie. 'Alexa's boyfriend.'

'Of course, of course.' In a world where I'd fought against the undead, hung out with space pirates, and found old corpses rotting away in their widows' kitchens,

I had learnt to be surprised by nothing. 'The boy is perceptive, I have indeed had visitors on the subject of your miraculous escape and not just the sort interested to see whether I'd like to convert to Jehovah's Witnesses as a result. I've had visitors from the afterlife and they're not exactly delighted about it, put it that way.'

I didn't think it was particularly beneficial to mention that it was only one visitor and that was one of Death's stooges.

'Can we see him?' asked Robbie.

'Visit Death?' I snorted. 'He didn't exactly leave a calling card with a contact telephone number, you know? That said, we could do with organising a visit, since your escapades are responsible for minor ripples cosmologically, like destroying the entire fabric of space and time.'

'Hey, don't try and pin the blame on me, technomage,' snarled Alexa. 'It was you who said it was possible! I wouldn't have even known I was going to die without you!'

'You were grateful for the information, if I recall right,' I retorted, but it was time to concede the point. 'Anyway, I know, I know. I hadn't considered the wider implications, had I?'

Most things I did involved contravening widely accepted laws of physics, chemistry and, sometimes, biology; however, they rarely had implications which threatened to destroy the entire existence of the real and meta-real universes. Well, semi-rarely anyway.

I motioned the lovebirds, if 'lovebirds' is the right term for what they were, to take a seat on the magic carpet, the plush fur of which was intended to make a comfortable seat for flights over deserts in the Middle East. Goodness knows what animal was slaughtered to line the carpet; I tried not to think of it during its frequent trips to repair shops and alchemists. Anyway, the carpet was normally more comfortable than any of the ancient (I hesitate to use the word 'antique') furniture that lined the room, which is why I seated Alexa and Robbie there to briefly fill them in on the findings of my various meetings with the psychopomp. The carpet started purring: I couldn't tell whether this was a feline indication of happiness or whether it had started running a motor.

'Listen, I was told the other day that if I was ever going to find out, see whether I'd truly escaped death, I couldn't run away. I'd have to look Death straight in the eye and say 'I've won, you've lost'. But I don't know whether I can do that now, I don't know if I can face it . . .' Alexa trailed off.

I looked at her and tried to break the news as gently as possible. 'We need to get back to rectifying this, Alexa. I'm sorry, I know it's not the result that any of us had in mind, but I've got to edit the footage again.'

I flicked open the Technonomicon and started entering the magic incantations required to access the computer. I say 'incantations', I was regularly told that the word was 'password' but that brought to mind images of the Riddle of the Sphinx and of ancient gatekeepers. The Warchestra footage had cut to a dramatic rendition of 'Toccata and Fugue in D minor', a piece of music so dramatically clichéd I suspected the Technonomicon of somehow doctoring the footage. Anyway, I had just opened the relevant file when Robbie cleared his throat and grabbed my arm.

'I want to go back too.'

I stopped my typing for a while and turned to face him. His face was determined, even defiant.

'Robbie,' I said, as gently as I could muster. 'That's very heroic of you. But we're not going back in time here, I'm just changing some of the details of what happened. I'm moving people and objects around. I can't just copy and paste you into the shot – it's history, not animation.'

Robbie stood up. 'Can I see the footage?'

I shrugged. 'All right.' I hit 'play' and showed him the grisly events unfolding. He wasn't looking at the foreground though, he was looking at the window at the front of the bank, light glaring off it constantly but still ensuring that the outside world was visible.

Suddenly, Robbie shouted, excited. 'There, hit pause.'

I did. Robbie pointed at the screen.

'There, look, at the window behind.'

I did, as did Alexa, who'd come forward to join him. There was, in the background, a youth with curly hair about to cross the road away from the bank. He was of medium height, perhaps, and in fact you could argue that he looked a lot like–

'That's me.'

'Oh, come on...'

'I'm serious. I was on my way to collect the day's papers, I get them from a place just down the road from there. I thought I heard some shooting that day, but figured it was probably the building work going on down the road – you know, men dropping bricks into skips and stuff. So I'm already in shot – I mean, in the picture. All you have to do is move me foreground.'

I looked over at Robbie. 'Why would I want to do that?'

'So that I can take the shot, not Alexa.'

I rubbed my forehead and ran my hand down my face. 'Robbie, I've just discussed what would happen if I did that. You know, the whole unravelling of the intended progress of space and time, all that jazz? I didn't just say that for my benefit, you know.'

'I know. But I'd like to hear it from the devil's lips, um, I mean, the horse's mouth. Er, I'd like to hear it from Death himself,' Robbie managed. 'That's what the last few months have been all about. Who says the world has to progress exactly as intended, anyway?'

I ran my fingers through my hair. 'All right, all right. But I'll tell you what. If this doesn't work, I'm out of this game, I'm going to gracefully retire from the show, exit stage right.' I turned back to the ghoulish laptop. 'Oh crap. The file's become Read Only. I've messed with it once too often I think.'

'So that means-'

'We're done for,' I finished.

I looked back at the Technonomicon, at the top right corner where the Camirror merrily shot footage of the whole room. I had no idea how it did that – it was as if it was recording from the corner of the room, rather than from a webcam. However, as I looked at it, an idea swam into mind. I looked up the earliest files from the Technonomicon's existence, back to the insomnia-plagued period in which I'd first discovered the power of remotely controlling the footage and ran them through the dreaded editing program.

Sure enough I was able to edit my own historical surroundings remotely, moving things around as if my house was in the middle of a poltergeist infestation.

'All I need to do is find out whether I can edit myself editing this footage,' I explained to Robbie and Alexa, as I attempted a drastic zoom. 'If so, I'll be able to edit you, Robbie, into the foreground so that, as you say, you can take the bullet for Alexa. You're aware of the consequences, though? This isn't you as you are now who I am editing here, this is you before any of this happened.'

'Which is before we met,' said Alexa, hollow. 'You won't know why you're doing what you're doing. None of this will have happened.'

'Alexa, you won't be able to avoid this either. You won't know you're going to die. If I knew I couldn't save you, I wouldn't have approached you in the street, I wouldn't have agreed to help you out. You'll be going into it blind.' I cursed internally the loss of revenue that this would result in, then felt guilty about doing so.

'There are also the moral implications,' I added. 'I mean, look at it from my point of view, Robbie: I'm basically sending you to your death here. Ironic, since the whole point was to *avoid* death where possible. Still, it's your call; as much as I hate to say it, it's going to have to be one of you.'

'It would still be the right thing to do, though, wouldn't it?' asked Robbie. 'It would be a heroic death in a life that was totally mediocre. I'm saving the world from total destruction here. But more importantly, I'm saving you. It'll be completely worth it.'

One life to save the universe. A bit of collateral for the world to be saved. One loss to prevent millions. I sighed. I had no choice. I made the necessary edits to the footage. My finger hovered over the 'Save' function.

'This is it guys. This version of the future ends right now. Say your goodbyes.'

Alexa turned to Robbie. 'Are you sure you want to go through with this?'

135

Robbie smiled. 'Hell, I didn't have any plans for the rest of my life anyway.'

'Even now? Now that we know that there is life after death, good and evil, that Death actually exists, that this isn't just some grand folly? You're not scared of those demons?'

'That pair of idiots from the ship? Strangely I don't think I'm that worried. Anyway, what are they going to do to me? A soul in an eternity of torment? Seems pretty similar to what I had here, to be honest.' Robbie realised too late the insensitivity of the remark. Still, it was too late to go back now.

Alexa tried to keep the hurt from her voice. 'You could call this off. Let me take the hit and you could go to acting school, make something of yourself . . .'

'And in twenty years time I'd look back on what I could have been and what I had become and I'd probably end up shooting myself anyway,' finished Robbie. 'At least this way, I don't die in some feeble and selfish way. I do some good, at least.'

'Saving my life, doing some good?' Alexa took Robbie in her arms now, on the verge of crying, which surprised Robbie: he'd always thought Alexa was tougher than this. But then who really is as tough as they appear? Does Mr T ever weep, or Chuck Norris?

'Call it off,' she murmured, stroking Robbie's hair, his cheek. 'We could try and make something of this, you know? There's still plenty of time left. I mean, as far as we know I'm immortal and you – you've got many years to live. We could get a place, have some kids, see more of the world...'

'And eventually you'd have to watch me die, remember that I'm not immortal?'

'Well, you know, that can be organised,' said Alexa, trying to keep the adolescent whining and pleading out of her voice and looking over at me opportunistically.

'Hey, don't bring me into this,' I said, holding my hands up. 'I've already got Death on my back, remember?'

'Listen, Alexa,' said Robbie, urgently. 'I could live a hundred years for you, I could pluck poppies from war-torn Afghanistan for you, I could save children from starvation and certain doom in a famine-stricken part of Africa for you, I could, I don't know, save a newborn litter of kittens from a burning house and we could take them all home and they could sleep on our bed, but there is nothing I could ever do for you that would be more romantic, more noble and more defiant than sacrificing my life for yours. You're clinging to this idea of happily ever after and I don't know whether that would exist. We've had so little time together, really. I don't think you could put up with me for much longer than this without my existence becoming a pain in your arse. Remember me like this: as someone who gave everything they had for you.'

'What can I say at this point, Rob?'

Robbie paused as the Warchestra switched to 'earlier today' footage of a French orchestra cynically using excerpts from the 'Romeo and Juliet' ballet on February 14.

'You don't have to say anything, Alexa. Just dance.'

'Dance? To this? I can't, it's been so long, I . . .'

At this point Robbie took Alexa's hands and indeed, they danced. What Robbie lacked in technique he was certainly making up for in terms of drama, whereas Alexa could definitely have been something had she perhaps

137

started earlier and maintained her discipline instead of skipping straight to the drunken has-been phase that she seemed to be in.

The ballet excerpt came to an end and the footage returned inevitably to some pundits, the insight of which I had come to regard with the same respect as a political commentator in the corner of a pub. Alexa and Robbie broke from each other, Alexa smiling as she did. By this point I just wanted to get on with it, before the fabric of space-time tore asunder and the entire history of time and space on the planet was ruined, which would have really scuppered my plans for the evening; and yet I was discreet enough to realise that minor issues like the Apocalypse could take a back seat to romance.

'There's so much I haven't said,' Alexa said. 'Where should I begin? What to tell you?'

'I dunno. Something which isn't some lame cliché? That'd be good.'

Alexa grinned. 'I suppose I should say thank you then. For saving my life. For showing me what life should be like.'

Robbie was smiling now. 'Hey, I said no lame clichés! But yeah, when we weren't being shot at, or being sick on ferries, we had some good times, didn't we?'

'Hehe, yeah. So, thank you for that. And . . .' she broke off.

'And?'

'Never mind'. They kissed. At the same moment my finger hit the 'Save' button and nothing after that mattered.

Chapter Ten

(I)

It was a frosty morning in November. Any pretence at sunshine was completely eliminated by the Arctic breeze that, having spent weeks exclusively haunting precincts and the lower levels of disused car parks, now broke free with a triumphant howl and smugly blasted throughout the town. Rampaging past billboards and bins, ignoring any attempts at buffering it and blowing straight into the bones of the morning's commuters. Such were the drawbacks of living near the sea: all the wind, but the salt air meant there was rarely any snow. Robbie didn't mind the snow: the whiteness all around him was close to the oblivion that he was aiming for and the feel of the snow under his feet, like sand mixed with cotton wool, pleased him. There was no snow today.

Robbie walked down the High Street, passing the suits piling into the magistrates' court for another session, past the side road the Salonium stood on, musing on a girl passing him by with a mixture of confusion and appreciation. Why was the girl wearing a short skirt in this weather, he wondered, before gloomily realising that the odds were that she was a prostitute. *This is the sort of thing Millie Kennedy used to sing about*, thought Robbie. *She'd understand why I feel the way I do, in a world that's gone to shit.*

Robbie continued, heading towards the newsagents who were set to lumber him with today's batch of free local rags that simply *must* be delivered by the end of the day. From behind him, two guys in suits and balaclavas cut in front of him, progressing with haste into one of the banks ahead of him.

Those men were Manny and Stevie, a pair of criminal desperadoes who were far from the good-looking rebels idolised in Hollywood movies. Manny had gone from shoplifting penny sweets as a child to robbing off-licenses and breaking into electrical stores. A motorbike crash had resulted in the loss of two fingers and a conviction for armed robbery had resulted in the loss of three years in prison. Stevie was more innocent, but for a promise that he had made to his sweetheart, an older lady by the name of Conzeula, that together they would travel the world, a promise that he knew full well would be empty, unless he robbed a bank or something.

Unless he robbed a bank . . . in fact yes, that's what he would do, he decided, tiring of a life living on the breadline. He had met Manny while awaiting counselling sessions for anger management, Stevie's undertaken voluntarily, while Manny's had been enforced by a court hearing after an incident in a department store. Stevie knew that Manny had a history of criminal activity, although Manny had neglected to mention that nearly all of it had ended in disaster and failure to procure the goods he'd come for. Stevie depended on Manny's experience and allowed him to plot the mission while he set about acquiring a pair of handguns from an underground terrorism network that he found online.

Meanwhile, in the bank, Alexa Ribiera had stopped off early before work to transfer some money over to her savings account and ensure that there would be enough remaining in her account to pay her bills until she was paid next week. Alexa had been saving for years, although had never been sure entirely why. She supposed that in the event that she was ever to have children she at least had a college fund for them; in the event that the father hung around long enough, she had a marriage fund; or in the event that neither of these things happened perhaps she would go crazy and travel round the world, visiting every continent, see some of the crazy far-out things that she'd heard about. Deep down, however, she knew that this was never going to happen. Ah well, at least she'd have a funeral fund.

Stevie had already checked that Conzeula would be home by the time the deed was done, so that he could set off on their voyage around the world that day.

Alexa went to the ATM machine, keying in her pin number.

Stevie and Manny burst into the bank, loudly declaring their intentions in a method that they had subconsciously stolen from the silver screen: in particular, they were reeling off the lame posturing of early Tarantino movies.

For reasons he couldn't understand, Robbie found himself drawn towards the bank. It occurred to him to check what his suicide fund was looking like today; screw it, it would only take a moment and the papers could wait.

'THIS IS A ROBBERY! EVERYBODY FREEZE!'

'I'M GONNA EXECUTE EVERY LAST MOTHERFUCKING ONE OF YOU IF YOU DON'T GET DOWN ON THE GROUND NOW!' screamed Stevie, baffling the bank's customers who'd just been told to freeze by the other idiot with the gun. 'DOWN!' yelled Stevie and this time they complied. 'NONE OF YOU MOVE!' He turned to one of the bank tellers. 'WHAT

141

ARE YOU DOING ON THE FUCKING FLOOR? GET UP AND GET US SOME GODDAMN MONEY!'

Manny shook his head. They'd only just started and already this wasn't going so good. Where did Stevie get the stupid idea of doing all the talking? They'd *been through this*, Goddamnit. He could see doubt spreading in the faces of the hostages (hostages? I guess they were) and some of them were edging towards the door and then some *other* stupid asshole walked through the door coming INTO the bank.

Robbie entered the bank and immediately wondered why he'd bothered.

Stevie was collecting money in a sack that he'd purloined for the occasion which could hardly have been more obvious if it had 'SWAG' or '$' written on it. Manny sighed. He was starting to lose control of the situation here.

Manny fired a shot. Everyone screamed, and half the customers started attempting to run. Manny fired another shot in the air and shouted, 'STAY WHERE YOU FUCKING ARE!' He pointed his gun randomly at some broad with hair everywhere, wearing some gross off-red suit, terrified, back to the ATM machine. 'I'm going to JUICE this bitch if you people don't start doing what you're goddamn told!' He was improvising here, trading on the assumption not that people wanted this old bitch's life extending but that they didn't want to see a horrible death on their way to work. It was only, what? He looked at the clock. 10.55am. Maybe it was their lunch break already, who cared? It wasn't even that busy in here and what did they have to benefit by keeping these people here? But they were doing it now.

142

Stevie was worried. He didn't want to see anyone shot any more than any of these people did. The poor fuckers were just doing a bit of banking, maybe checking their Christmas money, maybe moaning about the poor service received on the phone, but they shouldn't be dragged into this. He tried to concentrate on the money that the poor teller was sticking into his swag bag and tried to reassure himself with the thought that soon this would all be over and he'd be in the Southern hemisphere with the lovely Conzeula. Ah Conzeula! Even her name sounded like a poem.

Alexa was shitting herself. A lifetime of virtually nothing of consequence happening and here it was, the moment of her death. The thought swum into her mind that maybe in another universe she would have been approached by some sort of wizard who would have told her of this, unless . . . unless she wasn't going to die maybe? Hope springs eternal.

Robbie couldn't work out whether it was a good idea or not to mess with these guys, the situation was messed up. But they couldn't just go round pointing guns at women. Besides, what did he have to lose? He was an undiagnosed suicide watch. Would it be brave to intervene? Bravery be damned: if he died, he died a hero, but the point would be that he would be dead, that this ordeal of a life would finally be over.

'Come on guys, pointing a gun at a woman? That's pretty scummy even for a pair of scumbags like you,' he said, voice trembling, briefly cursing himself that he couldn't think of anything better than the repetition of 'scum'.

'Maybe you just want me to FIRE this gun, is that it?' screamed Manny, by now becoming exasperated, knowing the point of no return was on the horizon.

'What are you staring at? Come on, there's gotta be more than this! Open the safe!' yelled Stevie at the unfortunate teller.

'If you're gonna fire that gun at anyone, you can fire it at me,' Robbie shouted at Manny. Their voices, filled with artificial bravado, were loud, unnecessarily so; they echoed off the walls, rode over a wave of near-silence. The criminals, the teller and Robbie. Nobody else was moving, many were holding their breaths. Robbie started walking closer to Alexa.

'What the FUCK? You think I'm just screwing around here? I swear asshole, I'm going to do it!' screamed Manny, continuing to point his gun at Alexa. By now his aim was wavering, his arm trembling: he may have done a lot of bad things in his life but murder was not one of them. All of a sudden he found himself in the position where he wasn't offered a great deal of choice. Funny how that happened sometimes. He was swearing too often as well, he realised, a fallen log of a realisation on the tracks of his mind, derailing his train of thought. He promised his anger management counsellor he'd stop swearing. Mind you, he promised the screws in prison that he'd stop committing crime. Goddamned Stevie.

Goddamned Stevie, meanwhile, had stopped collecting and had turned to stare at the grisly situation himself.

Alexa dared to take two wavering steps to the side, but Manny held her in his target range.

Robbie had started feeling invincible. Doubt had obviously crept into the minds of these two morons. 'Do it then! Just don't shoot her!'

Manny thought of all the plans he had had with his share of the money. Go to Monaco, maybe, open a casino, marry a supermodel. Maybe go to Mexico and buy a boat and dive for treasure, who else was it who had that thought? Manny thought of whether any of this was worth bothering with, of a life which had gone completely haywire early on and whether he would ever, ever be able to fix it. Manny thought of Stevie and Conzeula and how happy they seemed to be and thought of this guy coming to save this stranger's life and how chivalrous that seemed to be and how unloved and cowardly and worthless he was in comparison. Fucking assholes, making me feel that way.

Manny screamed and fired.

Robbie dived into the line of fire and took the bullet in his upper shoulder, changing the trajectory of his dive in an unexpected way, the velocity sending him spinning, knocking him backwards and onto Alexa.

Alexa took the weight of Robbie and fell backwards, the back of her head hitting the ATM with full force, then hitting the floor hard, no carpet to break the fall, so dazed that she didn't even put her arms out to break the fall.

Stevie, realising that this was not what was scheduled, threw his balaclava down and joined the fleeing hordes as they raced out, hoping to pass as just another panicked civilian, a passing that worked well enough to get him the hell out of there. To Cemetery Drive. Five minutes, tops.

Robbie was collapsed on top of Alexa. His eyes caught the clock, staring down from the wall. 11.12. He'd heard that if you looked at a clock at 11.11, it meant your

145

guardian angel was looking down on you. He'd just missed it. Typical Robbie Adams, he thought. He looked down at his shirt, at his jacket, now stained red with blood. *I could do with some new clothes anyway*, he thought. He realised he was losing consciousness, his thoughts crashing together, images coming from everywhere. He thought briefly of Millie Kennedy, the singer. He remembered how her story ended now. Once upon a time she was the most famous singer to have had a career posthumously. More albums since death than 2Pac, more sales too. All of a sudden a duet with Cathy Lorenzo, a popular acoustic artist, had been released, and Lorenzo, in publicising it, had explained what a pleasure it was to meet Kennedy. The story unravelled from there and it turned out that Millie Kennedy had never existed, that she was a sham posed by a model, sung by a rotating cast of bland, wispy session singers and written by a pair of cynical producers. Once upon a time Robbie had thought that Millie was an inspiration to him, proof that your genius only comes to light once it had gone, but it had never existed at all, had it?

Robbie looked at the woman that he had just saved, looked into her eyes as they struggled to stay open. Suddenly a wave of images swam into view, images of the Ten Places To Die, images of him and this woman travelling through all of them, images of travelling with some weird group from the Victorian age, images of sex and of love. It seemed as if the Ten Places To Die weren't that good after all. But the woman on the other hand – suddenly he knew what she looked like naked, what she was like as a person and what she was like in bed, but the thoughts were deleting quickly. One moment he had a grip on an image of the New Guinea Cleavage and then it was gone, as if someone was recording over his memories. They weren't even memories, they were more like . . . more like . . . whatever the opposite was, a premonition or something, but it was a premonition of a life that did not, would not, could not exist.

Robbie groaned. This must be death. There was blood everywhere, he realised, like some third-rate horror novel. It wasn't just his, either, it was coming from this woman and all of a sudden he realised that he hadn't even managed to save her, that if anything, he had killed her himself.

'Useless, useless,' he managed. What derivative last words, his mind sneered.

One of the bank tellers, a blonde girl in her early 20s, rushed to attend to the two. Neither were looking likely to make it. 'Oh my God, are you all right?' asked the girl, force of habit involuntarily ejaculating the ridiculous question. 'We need to get an ambulance! Can I get anything, I dunno, bandages, water . . ?'

'You know, I never left a will,' the woman croaked. 'I'm the last in the line, there didn't seem much point. But do one thing for me. Make sure that what savings I have, go to this guy. I think the balance of those savings is still onscreen actually.'She turned to Robbie. 'You did your best . . . thank you. I love you, Robbie.'

Robbie forced out a breath. 'I love you too, Alexa,' he said. He had no idea how the two of them knew each other's names. Nor did Alexa, whose thoughts had toppled together in much the same way. Lucky guess, maybe. All of a sudden, she couldn't even remember that.

The world melted away in front of them in a way that's hard to describe unless you've ever been there. Imagine that the world we're living in now is like an old

VHS in terms of picture quality, then all of a sudden, you're experiencing a super high definition digital image. The real world – the physical world that we know of – suddenly seems harder, impersonal, dull and dead. The metaphysical plane that you have just entered is clearer, more intense, more beautiful and brighter, brighter by far. Of course, part of this is due to the fact that you're no longer seeing through your eyes – a brilliant piece of biological engineering though the eye may be, it's nothing compared to the intensity of the things that you see with your soul. The concept of sight is more powerful than the actuality of sight.

This was what near-death experiences meant by seeing a light at the end of a tunnel. Compared to the searing, blinding intensity of the light that everything was bathed in at this point, everything else is like walking through a darkened tunnel. The closer to death you come, the more the light increases.

The world of bank tellers and policemen and ambulances was no longer important, no longer even relevant. They were alone in a different sphere now, but this loneliness did not last for long, as a figure in black stepped into the fray, from what direction it was impossible to tell. If anything, the figure looked relieved.

'Finally we meet!' he enthused. 'You know, last time I came here there was nobody for me to collect. All of a sudden I've got two of you hanging around! What's this, I mean, you two come as some kinda 2-for-1 deal, what's that all about?'

Seeing as the physical world no longer seemed to matter and his body was in another world now, Robbie stood up. 'Are you Death?'

'Death?! Death, but not for you, Robert Adams. You can call me Zan!' said Zan. 'I fulfil most of the duties of Death though, yes: I escort the dead to the afterlife. Like that guy on the river Styx, you know that myth? Anyway, I'm rambling, I know, I'm just so glad to be here with you. Consider it an acceptance speech if you want. Now, if you don't mind getting out of my way, I'm here for Alexa Ribiera, thanks.'

'You mean you're not collecting me?'

'You? Nah. I've been to your death, you've got plenty of time yet.'

'So if this isn't it . . .Why did you go to my death?'

'Well, I say 'go', I asked the people who did . . .I was hoping to catch Alexa . . . look, this is a long story and I'm glad that you're here and all but this is more like a near-death experience for you, like one of those 'light at the end of a tunnel' jobs. For Alexa, though, I'm sorry, but this is the end.'

Robbie shook his head. 'No.'

'I'm sorry, what?' asked Zan.

'I'm not letting you take her eternal soul. I challenge you for it.'

Zan sighed. 'Oh, if it isn't the old 'challenging Death' routine, I don't know how many times I've heard this one. You know, it's kind of, er, presumptuous to challenge on someone else's behalf. I mean, how do you know Alexa even *wants* you to own her eternal soul? You're wasting your time, dude. But if you like, I can throw it to the floor. Alexa?'

Alexa was stood up now, looking beyond Zan and Robbie, dazzled by the light. She had a faraway look about her and at once Robbie realised that she was closer to Zan than to himself now, that she was on a different

149

existential plane altogether now. Her voice seemed to come from a million miles away, an echo from a distant memory. 'No, it's OK Robbie. This is my time.' She moved over to Zan, ready to take her place on the soul train. Zan guided her aboard. Robbie was aghast. Zan turned to Robbie.

'You see, this is the twist, this is the punchline, that nobody ever tells you about death. The afterlife, whether you go to Heaven or whether you go to Hell, is so much more intense, so much more wonderful and overwhelming and intense and magnificent than anything in your life. Nothing that has ever happened on Earth matters when you are in Heaven, in Hell, and you remember none of it. You become as one with the feelings that you experience there and you need worry for nothing, for eternity. How do you think you cope with leaving your loved ones behind? It doesn't even matter to you at this point, for you're as one with your afterlife and you are at peace. What did you think you would have, people playing harps and sitting on clouds?'

The light intensified. All of a sudden there was nothing, nothing at all, and Robbie was alone.

Then, darkness.

(II)

It was 11.15 when the doorbell rang at Conzeula Martinez's house.

'You were expecting someone else?' asked Stevie.

Conzeula looked beyond him and noticed his van parked across the road.

'No, I guess not,' said Conzeula. Why was she feeling so confused and out of sorts? Stevie was talking, but she wasn't hearing him. She tuned in again.

'. . . so what I'm basically saying is that we're going to set off now. You got everything you need?'

Conzeula nodded. She had been hoping for this journey for some time, although never seriously thought that Stevie would actually pull it off. The daring, the bravado! To think that, even in lean economic times, a pair of scoundrels like Stevie and Manny had been able to successfully pull off a large sale with a lucrative windfall commission bonus in it for both of them. So pleased was their company with this successful sale that they'd granted them the holiday leave that Stevie needed.

'Is Manny not with you?' she asked.

'Uh, no. Manny's caught at the office working on a couple of loose ends. He'll be OK, though. How about you, are you cool? You seem a bit distracted today.'

'It's probably nothing,' said Conzeula. 'It's just . . . Do you ever feel like someone's walked over your grave?'

Epilogue

(I)

It was different in Limbo, Zan noticed, as he wandered back to his soul train, checking the notifications on his never-ending To Do list. There was something a lot more austere about this place than usual, something more edgy and more unnerving, which, considering he was walking through an eternal, infinite place of moral and ethical neutrality, was saying something indeed.

Zan sighed. It seemed like there were always so many people to collect. One big adventure completed, but there were still people dying out there and it was his business to bring them to the next level. If one of those decided they could cheat Death, well, they picked the wrong psychopomp, baby. Because now he knew how to win that particular battle and he wasn't about to let that shit happen again.

He looked up. Somewhere in the distance (the distance?) was a figure on horseback, approaching him slowly. Unusually for Limbo the figure appeared to be shrouded in mist, almost as if he'd brought his own. Zan felt cold, although he didn't understand why. There was something about the mysterious stranger that made him uneasy.

He walked towards the trotting figure as the horse approached. On its back was a man with long blonde hair, dressed in white. He radiated an air of quiet authority and of terrible, infinite power. The absolute. The infinite. The definitive.

152

'You're different to how I'd expected you to look,' Zan said.

Death smiled, disembarking. 'Oh, come now. You forget that I'm the Angel of Death?'

Zan said nothing.

'It's Zan, isn't it? You'll have to forgive the antiquated mode of transport, but it does rather help to make a dramatic entrance on. Now, I do like to move among my, ah, representatives every so often, you know. Shall we move to the soul train?' Death spoke in a level baritone which, while a world away from the booming Shakespearean tones Zan had imagined, still cut through his soul like a highly-powered laser.

They stepped onto the soul train, which returned to its immaculate condition every time it was due to collect. Death sat down, examining the corners and contours of the coach.

'You know, I keep meaning to petition the Omniscience labs to do something about these coaches. I'm sure it would be a whole lot more efficient to simply use some form of teleport up here, don't you agree?'

'Yeah, I suppose,' Zan managed. 'I'm guessing it can't be done?'

'Well, apparently not,' shrugged Death. 'Still, it's a useful source of post-mortem recruitment and I expect you enjoy the role.

'I expect you've seen some interesting characters coming through this train,' continued Death, casually. 'That Alexa Ribiera sort, for one.'

Zan froze. Ah man, Death was omniscient too. He hadn't even thought about that, but it was so obvious; of course he was. Death would have to be, Death would have to know your time of death to the second and your

153

place of death to the square inch. Nobody could escape or outrun Death, not in the end at least, because Death knew. For Death, the rest was just waiting. And then if Death knew, then so did everyone else that Zan had been talking to in the afterlife. He had been played.

'Got into a pickle about that one, didn't we?' asked Death.

'If you knew about it, why didn't you do anything?' asked Zan.

'Well, as you've already realised, being in this position does have the benefit of a certain omniscience,' Death replied languidly. 'Of course you are aware of the importance of the particular mission and the importance of your success. We wouldn't want you destroying the fate of the planet and having to go to Hell, now, would we?'

'Um . . . no?'

'No. But as it happened, I knew that eventually you'd save the day. Naturally I would have stepped in if things had gone too far. If Alexa had blabbed her secret to anyone who had seriously believed her or if the experiment had been replicated to similar results, we would be looking at a potentially disastrous state of affairs. However, as it was, you pulled through and we are able to continue as normal.'

'So what happens now?'

'Well, that really depends on you, doesn't it?'

Death stepped past Zan and out of the soul train. He mounted his horse, ready to disappear into whichever infinity he lived in.

Before he departed, he turned back to Zan. 'One final thing, Zan. I've had psychopomps who've gone to Hell before from here. However, I've yet to have one who's made it to Heaven. Do you think you have what it takes to be the first?'

'Well, yeah, I hope,' said Zan, stumbling a little.

'So do I. You take care of yourself.'

(II)

Robbie woke up.

He was in a hospital bed, drip in his arm, things all over his body. His bullet wound bandaged up, his head too, presumably from the fall. His parents – his parents were there at his bedside.

'Robbie, I'm so glad you're OK,' his mum said.

'Hey Robbie, welcome back,' his dad greeted. 'A proper hero we've got in our family now then, eh?' He patted Robbie's shoulder, ignoring Robbie's involuntary wince. 'You know, I was just reading today's paper,' he continued, as if it was the most normal thing in the world for his son to have just woken up in hospital. 'They've just arrested one of the guys who did the job. Seems he'd been gallivanting around the world with his floozy, a woman called, uh, Conzeula. South America, the United States, you name it. Eventually they got caught on the way home, on a ship. They'd been to some ancient monument in New Guinea. Seems some woman called Anarchy recognised him from the news and alerted the ship's crew. Busted him at the docks. By the looks of it they didn't live a million miles away either – Cemetery Drive ring any bells for you?'

'No,' Robbie managed, weakly. Very little rang a bell at this point. He tried to remember the name of the woman involved, but the clouds of his condition obscured his memory.

'It's the first I'd heard of it too,' Adams Senior continued. 'Anyroad, the article also said that a local lawyer, Paul Kendall, is picking up the case and agreed to defend the scoundrel. Had this high-profile case a while ago but fallen on hard times of late apparently. Of course he asked us if you were available as a witness but, well, it didn't seem right in your condition. Still, I'm glad you're all right son, it was touch and go there for a while. For a couple of weeks we didn't think you'd make it.'

Robbie frowned. A couple of weeks? And one of the guys who did it had been around most of the world? 'How long have I been out?'

'Six months, son.'

'Six months?! For being shot in the shoulder?'

'The shot, the blood loss, the concussion. It's been rough. Still, you're on the right track now I think. That woman left you a fair sum of money, it has to be said. We could send you to acting school, see if we can't make something of you there, if that's what you want to do. You know, we spoke to your teachers. They said that they definitely saw you as an important character actor in the future – that you've definitely got a unique look. That's why you never got to play the lead. And you know the sidekicks, villains and supporting cast get all the good lines, anyway.'

His mother leaned towards him, concerned. 'We were looking in your room while you were here, Robbie. Making sure that it was ready for you when you came back . . . We found your diary, we found your list of places. Is everything all right with you? I mean, you're not actually planning to kill yourself, are you?'

Robbie looked out of the window, not at the birds singing in the trees and the children playing outside, no clichéd set-up like that at an NHS hospital, but he saw the sunset, heard the sounds of traffic and the banter of geezerish hospital porters. He looked at children's paintings and at an old man in the bed next to him, his wife silently holding his hand. He thought of the six months of his life that had disappeared and how he had come too close to annihilation, too close to futility. Suddenly Robbie realised there were still a million things he could do in the world and if that world didn't care about him, it was up to him to make it care. And as for wanting to commit suicide?

Robbie had forgotten that he ever had.

(III)

I was at Madison Square Garden enjoying the final Warchestra of the season between the New York Symphony Awesomeness and the San Francisco Supercomets, the latter of whom had recently employed ace cellist Marissa Mendoza for a spine-tingling Saint-Saens. I was running the Symph-assess software I had given to the sport and was unsurprised to learn that Mendoza was stealing the show so far. Of course, I was also enjoying the delights of creative chants like 'Your wind section blows' and the delights of the crappy fast food that American sport is synonymous with. Suddenly,

157

the hotdog tasted foul and artificial in my mouth – more so than usual, I mean – and the performance seemed to hang on a single note, which I assumed was not just suspense.

As time stood still, I looked round to see a figure in a black jacket approach me.

'I have a story for you,' Zan began.

Author's note

I hope the ending of the book makes the point clear, but just in case there is any confusion as to my actual leanings towards suicide, I should point out first and foremost that Robbie Adams' intentions in the book doesn't necessarily represent the best course of action and that the cast and crew of 'Cemetery Drive' do not support suicide as an option. For God's sake, tell someone if you're feeling inclined towards it and if your family or friends can't help, or if you're worried about someone you know following a similar direction, the Samaritans (0845 790 9090) or Papyrus (0800 068 41 41) are willing to listen.

Anyway, the existence of 'Cemetery Drive' and its genesis from overlong short story to full-length novel could not have been achieved without the support of those who've said nice things about my previous scrawlings. To them, I offer my thanks. (If you're as opposed to these sections as to the wearying thanks sections in CD booklets and Oscar speeches, I suggest you look away now.) Just some of those names: Brandon Downard, Danielle Crowter, John Halpin, Mark Hewitt, Mark Haines, Mark Everden, Matt Townsend, Michelle Douglas, Stefanina Hill, Steff Lawrence, Tom Simkins.

To the teachers who appreciated, indulged or at least tolerated my writing even at its most incomprehensible or self-indulgent, I am indebted and credit especially Chris Hawkes, David Higgins, John Rice and Simon Plowes.

Finally and most specifically, the people who've stood by me regardless of what percentage of my time has been swallowed up by either 'Cemetery Drive' or one of my various other efforts, who have listened to me attempting to explain the plot 4,000 times and who remain continually supportive of my efforts in literature and elsewhere, convinced of my writing skills even when nobody else was, and convinced of my personal strengths even when I wasn't.

As they've known me longest, from scribbles in notebooks to fanzines to university magazines to conceptual song cycles to books, and still been too nice to say it was all awful, my family must receive thanks first: to my nuclear family Christine, Gareth and Emily Wilson; to my grandmother Vivienne Dupree; to my grandparents Kathleen and Ray Meredith; to my ever-marvellous auntie Caroline Meredith and to my cousins Harriet and Graeme Meredith.

For their support and help on 'Cemetery Drive' I thank Tim Hirst for publishing, Jack Dexter for editing and proofing, Die Booth for many things but for the art most of all. And for being dumb enough to want to live with me during the crafting of this piece, for not sighing in despair as I waste hours of time over seven words, or a font, or a plot device, and for bringing me food, love and laughter, I am eternally indebted to Kyly Wilson and Lucy Radford. Finally, and inevitably, my own witch's familiar Cabaret, the jet-black moggy who, with his yowls for food and affection, reminds me that I do have a life away from this computer sometimes.

J.T. Wilson

April 2010

The publication of this novel was funded by pre-orders and Team Cemetery Drive extends eternal love and gratitude to:

Daniel Barry
Joanne Basnett
Cait Buckley
Daniel Charlesworth
Mike Cook
Ciaran Corkerry
Vivienne Dupree
Craig Faulkner
Cindy Garland
June Garner
Claudia Glazzard
Andy Gough
Tony Gough
John Halpin
Shaun Herrington
Stefanina Hill
Emily Hilton
Raymond Meredith
Jaci Peary
Lucy Radford
Melissa Reardon
Thomas Simkins
Stuart Simpson
Edward Sprake
Matthew Townsend
Justine Walshe
Sandra Wilson
Emily Wilson
Anthony Wilson
Gareth Wilson
Gerald Wilson
Christine Wilson
Kyly Wilson

Also from www.hirstpublishing.com

Lemon
By Barnaby Eaton-Jones

Spencer was an insignificant Data Input Operator and this suited him fine. However, when he is mistaken for someone actually significant, due to a mix-up by the Post Office, then his life becomes complicated. By complicated we're talking murder, sex, violence, car chases, beautiful women, and an annoyed fat cat (both of the feline* and big business variety). Spence didn't like complicated things and he was as far removed from being James Bond as Shakespeare was from being a hack plagiarist.

A week in Spence's life usually consisted of nothing more than dull, repetitive, time-wasting tedium. But, not this week. This week was going to be different and Spence wasn't going to like it one little bit.

* Just to add some extra zest to this 'Lemon', you can read all about Spence's love-hate relationship with his feline nemesis in 'Eric's Tale' at the end of the book.

Also from www.hirstpublishing.com

Flight Risks
By Douglas Schofield

Basel, Switzerland, February 2001 : Fifty-six years after the end of World War Two, Switzerland's bankers finally agree to release 21,000 dormant accounts left behind by Jews who died in the Holocaust. Claims from the victims' heirs pour in from across the world...

New York and Washington, September 2001 : The Twin Towers fall. The Pentagon burns. Western democracies scramble to meet a deadly new threat...

Victoria, Canada, October 2001: For legal secretary Grace Palliser, the post-911 media circus is just background noise. Grace is too busy with the unholy mess she calls her life. But when she stumbles on evidence of a vast international fraud, her life gets a whole lot messier. Framed for murder and desperately searching for the evidence that will clear her, Grace flees across the continent to New Orleans, then to the Florida Panhandle, and finally to a small island in the northwest Caribbean. Hot on her trail is a corrupt former cop with a simple assignment - to Kill Grace Palliser.

Match Day
By Darren Floyd

A comic thriller about three people having three different days, on the same match day in Cardiff. Cathy is a woman disappointed in life when her dream turns into a nightmare, and mires her with debt which she doesn't have a hope of paying off. Suddenly she is offered a chance of a new life in Australia, but first she must take a desperate gamble... Martin is a bitter policeman with decades on the job, and a shameful secret in his past. He finds himself in events that he could never anticipated. Leigh is a supporter; he just wants to get into see the match. Unfortunately he gets split up from his mate who has his ticket. He finds himself alone in a city full of sports fans. Now if he can only find a ticket... Gradually these three people's paths collide, and none of their lives will be the same again...

Also from www.hirstpublishing.com

Look Who's Talking
By Colin Baker

To many, Colin Baker is the sixth Doctor Who; to some, he is the
villainous Paul Merroney in the classic BBC drama The Brothers.
But to the residents of South Buckinghamshire he is a weekly voice
of sanity in a world that seems intent on confounding him. Marking
the 15th anniversary of his regular feature in the Bucks Free Press,
this compilation includes over 100 of his most entertaining columns,
from 1995 to 2009, complete with new linking material. With fierce
intelligence and a wicked sense of humour, Colin tackles everything
from the absurdities of political correctness to the joys of being an
actor, slipping in vivid childhood memories, international
adventures and current affairs in a relentless rollercoaster of
reflections, gripes and anecdotes. Pulling no punches, taking no
prisoners and sparing no detail, the ups and downs of Colin life are
shared with panache, honesty and clarity, and they are every bit as
entertaining and surreal as his trips in that famous police box... for a
world that is bewildering, surprising and wondrous, one need look
no further than modern Britain, and Colin Baker is here to help you
make sense of it all, and to give you a good laugh along the way.

Also from www.hirstpublishing.com

Self Portrait
By Anneke Wills

This is a moving, witty and candid account of a fascinating life among the talents who defined the swinging sixties. Appearing in ground-breaking television from an early age, Anneke Wills was one of the busiest actresses of the 1960s – her role as Polly establishing a template for one of television's most iconic and prized roles – the glamorous Doctor Who girl. This is a beautifully written story of a unique childhood, life at the heart of swinging sixties London, and a turbulent marriage to a leading actor. Anneke's life revolved around the eccentrics, actors, film-makers, painters, designers, poets, satirists and drunks who were changing the world. She counted among her friends the leading lights of the time – from Peter Cook to Sammy Davis Jnr. Illustrated in full colour with previously unseen photographs and Anneke's own drawings and paintings, this is the story of a rich and colourful life, and the growth of a truly remarkable woman.

Also available:
Naked, by Anneke Wills
(volume 2 of her extraordinary autobiography)

**All Aliens Like Burgers
By Ruth Wheeler**

Young, polite and intelligent Tom Bowler has barely ever ventured out of the small English town where he grew up. So when he applies for a job in a fast food restaurant at a "local" service station during his gap year he is rather surprised to discover that the vacancy is in fact based on Truxxe, a planetoid stationed between local galaxies Triangulum and Andromeda. Hes surprised further still to find himself becoming friends with a purple alien and that he has strange feelings for his android supervisor, Miss Lola. Tom soon discovers that Truxxe has many hidden secrets - just what makes it so special? And why is its terrain so rich and varied that it can be used for fuelling such a diverse variety of intergalactic spacecraft? What are the Glorbian space pirate brothers Schlomm and Hannond plotting? And just what is it that they put in those burgers?

For teenage readers, from
www.hirstpublishing.com

One Night Under Castle Moor
By Mark Leyland

A spooky adventure for 12-14 year-old readers

The Martens have to be the coolest craziest bunch of kids ever. Steve is new in town, the friends he's made here are all Martens and he's desperate to join. But first they've set him a test, to spend the night in a kind of stone cellar up on the moors - and he's not that wild about tight places. Luckily hard-girl Sophie volunteers to keep him company, but they find out too late about the Curse of Doom Castle. The story is that a knight was once left to starve to death in that cellar and he's supposed to return every year, at midnight on the day he died, to take revenge on anyone he finds there. And guess what day it is!

Another fast-moving scare from the award-winning author of Slate Mountain.

For teenage readers, from
www.hirstpublishing.com

Georgie Jones...
and you thought your family was weird!
By Nicky Gregory

An exciting adventure for 10-13 year-olds

The last thing that Georgie Jones wanted was to have to spend her
Christmas Day with Dan Parsons - unknown entity from school.
However, when Dan gets sucked into a 'loophole' transporting him
to the land of Molitovia, Georgie is quick to follow! How could she
possibly have known that her arrival in this strange land was far
from coincidence? In fact, if what they said was true, it was not only
her birthright to be here - it was her destiny! But should she really
believe that she was one of them? They all seemed to have their own
reasons for wanting her there and the only person Georgie had to
help her try and make sense of it all was Dan, who was not exactly
taking the situation very seriously! Georgie had a lot to learn - and
most of it about her own family!

Find Hirst Books on Facebook
Get regular special offers, promotions, all the
latest news, and connect with our authors.

**And if you've enjoyed this book, why
not enter a short review on the
Cemetery Drive page of our website?**

www.hirstpublishing.com